REQUIEM FOR A POSTMAN

REQUIEM FOR A POSTMAN

MARGARET PRESS

Carroll & Graf Publishers, Inc.
New York

Copyright © 1992 by Margaret Press

First Carroll & Graf edition 1992

Carroll & Graf Publishers, Inc.
260 Fifth Avenue
New York, NY 10001

Library of Congress Cataloging-in-Publication Data

Press, Margaret L.
    Requiem for a postman / by Margaret Press. — 1st Carroll &
Graf ed.
        p.   cm.
    ISBN 0-88184-750-X : $18.95
    I. Title.
  PS3566.R38R47   1992
813'.54—dc20   91-28417
                                                       CIP

Manufactured in the United States of America

For
the inhabitants of Salem Willows,
especially,
Stan and Sara

AUTHOR'S NOTE

I wish to acknowledge with sincere gratitude the help and support of the following people:

Adrianne Lilley, Sara Press, William Story and members of his summer 1990 class, William Press, Ella Roberts, Margaret Leighton, Robert Leighton, Jeffrey Howell, Roselyn Teukolsky, Billie Press, Brigette Sullivan, Paula Press, Katherine Dreher, Doris Ricci, Charlotte Thompson, Jim Madsen, Andrea Caggiano, Paul Gangi, and Rav.

For their generosity and expertise, Detective Sergeant Paul Tucker, Detective Sergeant Conrad Prosniewski, Detective James Page of the Salem Police Department, Criminal Investigation Division; also Detective William Jennings; Detective Mary Butler; former park officer, Sergeant Peter Gifford; Medical Examiner, Dr. Albert Shub; John P. Noyes; Tom Campbell of the U.S. Postal Service, Salem, Mass.; Dennise Munroe; Mary C. Wilson; Bob Craig; Stanley Anderson; Sara Press for Latin translations. Any and all errors are my own.

I also thank Hector Berlioz, W.A. Mozart, J. Brahms, G. Verdi, and Andrew Lloyd Webber for their inspirational renditions of the Requiem Mass. And J.S. Bach for his Magnificat. And the anonymous baritone (actually a tenor), who hopefully is now doing what he wants.

With the exception of Monument Road, Salem Willows is, I am happy to report, real. The people and events are not.

REQUIEM FOR A POSTMAN

Prologue

There is nothing deader than a dead dog. The hair lies oily and flat against the skin. The chest is deflated and the carcass is a prisoner of gravity until the stiffening makes it rigid. One force or another. But never again its own. Ray Bishop lifted what was once his wife's spaniel into a black Hefty bag and lowered it into the hole behind the garage.

Thinking that maybe the bag wasn't such a good idea, he extracted it, finally. To restore a bit of ceremony, he went into the kitchen and got the last of the Milk-Bones from the cupboard under the sink. He returned to the graveside. Bishop shook the box solemnly over the dog. The only sound was of the bones sliding off the cardboard. They made no noise as they fell upon the fur.

While his wife Christmas-shopped, Bishop shoveled back the dirt. He was lucky the ground had still been soft for December. When he was done, the yard restored, shovel put away, he returned to the kitchen to wash his hands and to weep.

Chapter 1

Exaudi orationem meam;
ad te omnis caro veniet.

Hear my prayer,
unto you shall all flesh come.
—Psalm 65:2

"Hate it when the flies get to them before we do." Detective Sergeant Gabriel Dunn had taken a few minutes accommodating himself to the stench in the men's cottage before approaching the body.

From his post at the doorway, the patrolman grunted in a barely audible response, "Gotta be the worst part of dying, huh? Maggots in your eyes."

Sergeant Dunn let out his breath slowly. "Like they're looking up at you and saying, 'where ya been?' " he said. "Guy's missing two weeks and he turns up three hundred yards from his house. You sure it's him, Brian?"

Officer Brian Hurd had been the primary officer called to the scene. The Willows, which included the park, was part of the twenty-one car beat, Hurd's for the past six years. He knew the residents well. Stable, quiet, a lot of vets. Not much turnover. "Yeah, I'm sure. His face is pretty distinctive. Even with all the uninvited guests." Hurd always sounded like he had laryngitis.

Puffy and distorted from decay, faces took on a new kind of distinction. Hardly a noble fate, Dunn thought. Entombed in the men's room of your local park with insects in your face. Perpetuating the original assault. Prolonging the demise. Somehow you're not done dying until someone with two legs discovers you. The detective looked at his watch. Twelve fifty-three P.M., Monday, March 19. *Well, you're dead now, Mr. Bishop. Real dead.*

Dunn swung the stream light around the chamber. Fixtures and corners, caught as if in oncoming headlights, were bathed in rusty illumination. High windows on either side would afford a cross breeze without their winter shutters, but now offered no air, no relief, and no light. Across from the half dozen stalls was a row of urinals. At the end of the room were a couple of sinks and a foggy mirror. In front of the sinks was the former postman, stretched at an angle and lying on his back. The cement floor between the threshold and the corpse looked scraped clean and free of debris.

The thirty-six-year-old detective sergeant turned his attention again to the dead man. Male, Caucasian, looked to be in his late fifties, early sixties. About a hundred and seventy, he guessed, despite the distension, and five seven or so. Dunn was pretty used to estimating heights from lengths in this job. He bent down and shone the light into what was left of the eyes. The State might have to pull in an entomologist to help place the time of death.

Dunn crouched, mindful of where he placed his feet. Careful prodding revealed no stiffness. Most likely it was long gone. The discoloration from early stages of decomposition masked any traces of postmortem lividity. A single wound, forceful enough to break the skin, adorned the left temple. The head was turned slightly to one side, and behind the left ear, the hair was matted with dried blood. No pool blemished the floor below, however. Only a brown smear testified to this off-season intrusion.

Not much else he could check until the lab arrived. Finally he stood up. "Talk to me, Brian."

Hurd opened up his notebook. With rasping voice, the patrolman recounted his initial observations, the time of the call, and everyone's movements since his arrival. A Mr. Arnie Costa, supervisor from the Department of Public Works, had opened the door, but had touched nothing else. "The medical examiner's on her way. State's been notified."

Dunn joined him in the doorway. "I want Mr. Costa to show us exactly where he stepped. Also, let's get elimination prints of his hands and shoes before he disappears. Where is he now?"

"I told him to stick around."

Dunn stepped outside where cruisers were gathering like flies. He took several lungsful of fresh air. Despite the overcast, it actually felt like spring, smelling of green and tasting of the sea. The audience was assembling. The local dicks were cooling their heels. The State, in its own good time, would be making their entrance shortly, moving in with the faint threat of higher jurisdiction, changing the scene into The Scene. When the invasion was over, it would be Dunn's case. But for the next two hours, he would be tripping over Crime Prevention and Control guys from the DA's office, busy trying to strike a perfect balance between sounding helpful and being patronizing. The photo and lab team would come in, be useful, then return to Boston to let the spoils age.

Yellow crime-scene tape had been strung around the trees nearest the cottage. Officer Paul Szymanski, who had been Hurd's backup, was practicing some measure of crowd control on the growing public. Half the Salem Police Department were milling around unsupervised waiting to get their look, with vehicles and manpower still pulling up like latecomers to the Christmas ball. Dunn began to commandeer every cop who felt important enough to step out of his cruiser. Rather than watch in frustration as the scene was trampled, he had his guests organize a grid search of the park. When the chief pulled up, Dunn exercised the full extent of his authority in the case and sent him out for coffee and doughnuts. A symphony of radios chorused like hens from the marked units clogging the parking lot.

Before the searchers had a chance to destroy it, Dunn started to check out the cordoned area himself. He circled the cottage slowly, inspecting the window shutters for signs of force, and scanning the ground for loose rocks or places a weapon might have been discarded. He was halfway around when Hurd's cracking voice called out, "Lab's here."

Behind them came the doughnuts, and behind the doughnuts came the medical examiner. The waiting was over. After the formalities and pleasantries, Dunn hung around until everything of interest had been photographed and listed. Not much of a haul; this scene was pretty unyielding. While the lab set about rehashing and bracketing, the detective went to find Arnie Costa.

On the other side of the parking lot, the Salem Willows Park arcade, known locally as "the line," was still closed for the season. Faded orange rowboats, rentals from Memorial Day through late October, were stacked between Hobbs's popcorn stand and Salem Lowe's Chow Mein. The park's main footpath was now littered with dead leaves, devoid of its popcorn boxes and summer attire, and the kids who, six months ago, crouched down to peel gum off the sidewalk.

The grounds embraced the eastern tip of the Salem Willows promontory, which separated Beverly and Salem harbors. A few green gazebos were elevated to give ocean views on all sides that once were idyllic. Nowadays, the Beverly shoreline to the north was branded with a pair of golden arches. To the southwest, the towering stacks of the New

England light plant, which occupied a sizable chunk of the Willows, intruded upon each vista.

Except for the small cleanup crew from the DPW, the park had been still that morning. The pair of swans, which before every St. Patrick's Day briefly graced the harbor periphery, were late this year. Weeks ago the last of the Canada geese had left. The cormorants were a month off. Only a few gulls were in attendance, and the gray ducks of assorted varieties known to the hunters. And there were the dogs.

The men's and ladies' cottages took up discreet residence close to the road, hidden from view by the graceful willow trees for which the peninsula was named. Green shutters covered the high, frosted windows, protecting against the winter's fury. "Closed" signs adorned each door. The water had been shut off, and dozing mosquitoes clung to the damp tiles within. By noon the temperature had hit fifty and the dogs had come sniffing round the men's-room door, painted green and bolted shut.

The dogs of the Willows came with every season. Like the ducks, they needed no justification and had unknowable purposes. Some followed daily schedules more predictable than the commuter train, which rumbled incongruously across the Beverly Harbor bridge into Salem each hour. Dogs everywhere patrol the earth with a narrow but acute sensitivity for things gone wrong.

Two in particular, a stringy brown collie and a small black all-American, made the rounds of the entire Willows each morning, finishing down at the park around ten. Mondays took them longer because it was trash pickup day. It was just after noon when they had arrived at the cottage door. Approaching the threshold, the smaller dog had nosed his way up to the gap at the bottom of the door and had started to whine. Finally it was the collie's barking that had attracted the attention of the Public Works crew.

*   *   *

Dunn located the DPW men in the tiny amphitheater at the far end of the park. Perching on the backs of the benches, they were talking quietly among themselves. Work had come to a complete stop. They had collectively decided that to best lend assistance to the police, nothing more on the entire grounds should be touched. Sitting by himself a few rows over, the white-haired supervisor stared at the empty stage where last summer he had watched the Air Force band perform a night of military fanfares. Dunn went over and sat down beside him.

"The officer said I could come down to the station for the prints later," Mr. Costa announced, a bit defensively. He wasn't about to detach himself from the bench.

"That's fine, Mr. Costa. Just wear the same shoes." Dunn offered him a doughnut.

The man shook his head. "I lost it in there, you know."

"I know," Dunn answered. "Understandable. Can you tell me exactly what you saw and did?"

"I hardly went in. I could smell it as soon as I turned the doorknob. Swung it halfway open and saw him."

"There was no light."

"The light from the door. I could see his foot. And I could hear the flies. That was what got me . . . the buzzing."

The detective considered asking him how he knew the foot was dead, but Mr. Costa's face was as blanched as his hair.

Leaving the supervisor to his recuperation, Dunn went back and found Officer Szymanski. "Paul, I'd like you to notify the wife. Call in and find out where she works. Make sure she's taken home. I'll be by to talk to her when I'm through here."

"You don't need her here for identification?"

"Brian is good enough for the moment. I don't want her seeing him like this."

*   *   *

Mrs. Ray Bishop had reported her husband missing on March 5. Only three years away from retirement, he was not of an age where wandering off would have been a credible explanation. Nor had anyone been able to imagine a reason why he would willfully disappear. Every weekend for thirty-five years, he had poured his soul into his house and garden. Energy and affection that might have been absorbed by children had been diverted into flower beds with clay animals, chronically trimmed lawn and hedges, and a home out of *Family Handyman*.

Everyone had known Bishop was counting the months. His job with the post office had become barely tolerable, as happens when one loses interest. Nevertheless, he had seldom taken sick leave, and had arrived punctually for each shift. But on the fifth of March, Bishop had not shown up. Retirement had come early.

After eight years as detective, Dunn took his corpses seriously. Unlike Boston, where homicide is weekly fare, death in Salem tends toward natural causes. But once or twice a year, it is helped along by someone who benefits from the demise. Dunn's job was to find those who had helped. He was still twenty years away from the ulcers and heart disease that the job promised in the end. Not yet at the age where cynicism and frustration would cripple him, but enough years of good police work to have acquired some measure of competence, wisdom, and respect. His time on the street notwithstanding, Dunn often felt that his acceptance by his fellow officers was based more on his not disgracing himself in softball than on his investigative or supervisory prowess. Despite a lanky runner's build, Dunn was not excessively athletic. The Salem Police Department softball team was one of the more perilous facets of his job.

Neither was he overly erudite. Mild dyslexia diagnosed late in his childhood had prevented him from becoming a strong reader. Dunn was keenly aware of the cost. Throughout his life he had gravitated to more comfortable channels of communication. Music was his passion; pounding on his upright piano was his release.

Dunn was not illiterate. He had, with difficulty, learned to read and to compensate well, struggling his way through a bachelor's degree at a local college. On his first police case he had scrambled a license number, wasting two days of his time and nearly costing him the case. Since then he had been meticulous; every note he took, every report he read, was done laboriously and accurately. At home the mental effort of the day left the detective drained and aversive to the written word. Dunn had never subscribed to a newspaper, except during the four years of his ill-fated marriage. He never read owners' manuals or assembly instructions. Much of his early sleuthing habits came from having to assemble patio furniture or set his VCR up for Timer Record, all without print.

The men from the lab were winding up. The chemist had been unable to raise any recent traces of human blood, visible or occult. A few fresh prints had been obtained from the doorjamb, quite possibly Mr. Costa's. A couple of footprints. No obviously significant evidence had been found in the room, aside from the cadaver. They had collected a small amount of trash, including a couple of cigarette butts, which now occupied a plastic bag destined for Boston. After the photographer finished his last roll, the three packed up their equipment and turned the cottage over to the medical examiner.

Dunn had worked with Dr. Gloria Mei before and knew she didn't like to be crowded. He watched quietly from the doorway while she finished conducting her examination by flashlight. Hurd peered over his shoulder.

"Wouldn't the scarcity of blood indicate he died immediately?" Hurd asked hoarsely. Hurd hoped to make detective someday.

Dunn shook his head. "Oh, this guy bled all right. He just didn't bleed here."

Dr. Mei emerged from the cottage and removed her latex gloves from tiny hands. At five ten, Dunn towered over her by nearly a foot. The guys from the DA's office liked to call her Dr. Ruth. She tucked her flashlight into her kit with an air of finality.

"Sorry, Gabriel. We won't be able to post him until to-morrow . . . we're so backed up."

"Can't get good help nowadays?" he asked.

"Not at sixty-five dollars a case."

"What can you give me now, Gloria?"

"Without the lividity I can't tell yet if he was moved after death. May know from the post."

"How about the wound?"

"For now, blunt weapon to the left temple. No other obvi-ous wounds or signs of fighting. Nails are clean. Some scratches on the backs of his hands. I'd say he was dragged. Back of his trousers looked dragged, anyway. The jacket was clean, though. Any witnesses I should talk to?"

Dunn shook his head. "How long's he been dead?" he asked.

"Difficult. Depends how long he was out in the freezing temperatures. Rigor mortis has completely passed. The cold has slowed down the decomposition." She looked out toward the parking lot. "By the way, I sent Rescue away. Who called for them? You have a new beat man?"

"I believe Mr. Costa notified every city department in the book. You think it's OK to dismiss the harbormaster, too?"

"Mr. Bishop has been pronounced. You can dismiss the dog constable if you like. I'll call you when we've scheduled the post."

Dunn gave her a smile. "Thanks. Don't spend it all in one place, Gloria."

Dr. Mei returned to her car and called for an undertaker. She contacted Salem Hospital to alert them a corpse was arriving, that it should be held for autopsy in the morning. Then she was gone.

Dunn watched while the body was removed. Then he took a closer look at the floor. Some effort had been made, apparently, to obscure the killer's footprints. The concrete immediately surrounding where the corpse had lain was smudged. Whoever it was had probably worked in the dark or by flashlight, however, so there was still a possibility the lab might have salvaged some remnant. Finally he turned his attention to the door and padlock. Hurd was still stationed at the threshold. Dunn asked him about the state of the lock when the police had arrived. DPW had come up with a key and had themselves unlocked it prior to calling the police.

"Are they sure it was locked? Not just, somehow, closed?" Dunn asked.

"Absolutely. They tried to open it while they hunted down Mr. Costa. He had the key."

Dunn made a mental note to talk to Mr. Costa again, about when these cabins were locked up for the winter and who had keys besides the park officer and DPW. Then he took a close look at the hasp. A cheaply installed hasp can make a joke of even the best of padlocks. And sure enough, this hasp was a riot. Each piece was attached to its destination by a couple of wood screws. Or rather, wood *screw*, in the case of the piece on the door. One screw was gone. Dunn looked slowly down to the ground, letting his eyes trickle down the doorjamb half expecting to see it caught in some crevice. He crouched down and probed the cracks around the threshold with his Swiss Army knife. Unsatisfied, he straightened up and, taking a small pen light from his pocket, gave his full concentration to the remaining screw. The head, like the hasp, had been painted green once, probably in this decade. Leaning closer, he could see the fresh signs of a screwdriver's work. This screw had been removed recently. Faint markings, scratching off tiny bits of paint, also were visible around the second hole. Whoever had come here had removed two screws and replaced one. The blond detective, hair the color of hay, dropped his head for one last search.

Chapter 2

Kyrie eleison
Christe eleison.

Lord, have mercy
Christ, have mercy.
—Requiem "Kyrie"

Across the harbor, Dover Landry had gone back to her room on Rantoul Street during a late lunch break. Hauling out a manila folder from the chest by her bed, she dumped the contents onto the linoleum camping table set up in the middle of the floor. From the pile before her she extracted a list of names and addresses. From her jacket pocket she produced a small piece of notepaper with Cabot Street Antiques printed on the top, followed by a string of penciled phone numbers. The young woman laid it to one side and began running her finger down the list of names. Near the bottom of the page she came to Bishop. She stopped. Fishing out the pencil from the other pocket, Dover slowly checked it off.

The Salem Police Department occupied a condemned building on the corner of Central and Charter streets, four blocks from the nearest witch museum. The inadequacies of the facility extended to what served as the parking lot. The short block of Central Street had been bricked at one end, dissuading traffic and corraling cruisers during shift changes into a coagulated and confused flock at the front door. There were reserved spaces for the Criminal Investigation Division, the Juvenile officer, Patrol supervisor, Executive officer, and Chief. There were no spaces for the public.

Dunn swung the recently seized blue Camaro into one of the spaces marked CID and killed the engine. He went upstairs to the detectives' office, rang the officer in charge and asked him to locate Detective Jake Myles. Then he pulled the missing-person file on Ray Bishop. He spread the contents out on his desk. Included were assorted statements obtained from family, neighbors, and friends two weeks earlier. According to those who knew him, Bishop had had no known enemies, relevant medical problems, was not on drugs, owed no money, was not cheating on his wife. No recent despondency, no prior history, or trouble at work. His wife knew of no unusual phone calls at the house. Last seen wearing a green jacket, reported by a neighbor. A missing-person bulletin was entered into the National Crime Information Center computer Monday afternoon, March 5, with a separate entry on his Lincoln. The one on the vehicle was taken out later the same day when it turned up at the Salem commuter rail station. A hard copy of the BOLO on the car was stuck in the back: *Be On Look-Out . . . operator of this car is possibly an involuntary missing person. Please hold for prints and notify Det. J. Myles, Salem PD. . . .*

A neighbor down the street at No. 55 had once been involved in an altercation with Bishop over a dog, ending up with some yelling and shoving and the threat of a lawsuit. Others who lived on Monument Road had confirmed that Bishop's dog had been a nuisance since the day it had arrived, but few wanted to arouse his notoriously quick temper over it. The neighbor immediately to the east, No. 94, the

last house in the row, had had a dispute over the placement
and height of a fence separating the two properties. The
picture that emerged was of a man who might have had no
mortal enemies, but who certainly had few friends.

The OIC rang Dunn's extension.

"He's still in court, Gabe. Want him beeped?"

"Nah. I'm going back out to Monument Road. I'll call in
after four. Give him a message when he next checks in. Ray
Bishop's been found. He's cold."

Officer Szymanski had visited Coleen Bishop before Dunn
arrived. The Bishops' Cape house was near the end of the
row lining Monument Road as it approached the park. Separating the quiet neighborhood from the park was a stretch of
no-man's-land, a tiny urban wilderness courtesy of the
nearby power plant.

Most of the homes on the street consisted of Capes and
bungalows, originating from the late forties and fifties. From
World War II through the Korean War, the city of Salem,
in a patriotic and appreciative gesture, had subsidized house
lots along Monument Road for veterans of the wars. Shortly
after returning from Korea, Bishop had secured a lot across
from Collins Cove for just over a hundred dollars. He hired
the architectural firm of J. Gerrison in September 1955, and
built his dream house at 92 Monument Road. The small
Cape, ideally suited to a couple without children, took advantage of the water view but was otherwise modest. Most of
its charm lay in the potential it held for the retirement years.

Coleen Bishop was nearly twenty years younger than her
husband. She was his second wife. Slender, carefully
dressed, she was far from dowdy, not quite what Dunn had
expected. Her face was blotched from crying. For a moment
she stood with uncertainty in the entrance hall, as if she were
a stranger in the house and waiting for guidance. When the

detective suggested they sit down, Mrs. Bishop led him into the kitchen and motioned toward a chair.

Dunn hated talking to the widows. Often their reactions were significant; they were usually the primary suspect. But when their grief was sincere, he found himself making the difficult choice between roles of observer and participant. He needed information from them. Yet he watched his words prick and tear at their wounds when what they needed was compassion.

Mrs. Bishop wasn't quite ready to sit down, needing to busy herself first with coffee preparation. While he waited for her, Dunn studied her back. The woman's hair was strawberry-blonde and short. Curly, probably permed. A red wool skirt topped with a splashy flowered blouse, out of tune with the occasion. Turquoise running shoes with white accents. She must have been brought home from work.

Finally the woman set down two mugs and lowered herself onto a chair. Dunn noticed that her earrings were identical to a pair his ex-wife used to wear. Small studs with green stones to match her eyes.

The police had questioned her extensively when her husband was reported missing. Dunn went over the story with her again.

On Thursday, March 1, after a quarrel with her husband, Mrs. Bishop had left for a four-day visit with her sister in Gloucester. She then had talked briefly to him early Friday evening. She had tried calling again over the weekend without success. Returning Monday around noon, she had been alarmed to find newspapers uncollected in the driveway. Mail had littered the floor inside the front door below the slot. She then contacted his supervisor at work and learned that he had failed to show up. After trying a few friends, she had finally phoned the police. Bishop's car had been located four hours later in the parking lot of the train station. No other trace of him had been found. From that point on, life ceased

to be private, and the quiet desperation of a failing marriage
turned into the foreboding threat of widowhood.

"Mrs. Bishop, do you know of anyone who might have
had reason to kill your husband?" Dunn asked. She shook
her head and dabbed her reddened eyes with a wadded-up
Kleenex. Dunn watched her carefully.

"Any idea why he would be down at the Willows?"

She responded: "He walked down there nearly every day.
Even though he walked so much on the job, he still liked to
go down there." She looked up. "Do you think maybe,
maybe he was mugged, Sergeant?"

"We don't know yet. Mrs. Bishop, I know you've been
asked these questions before, but we need to go through it
again. When you returned on Monday, what else besides the
mail and papers struck you as unusual?"

"The garbage hadn't been put out. He usually puts it out
. . . used to . . . on Sunday night."

Dunn said: "Think carefully. What was your first impression when you walked in? That he had left on a trip, or just
on an errand, or that he hadn't intended to leave at all? Think
about whether lights were on, doors locked, dishes cleaned,
things like that."

She pulled herself together and thought for a minute. "I
thought he had gone to work at first, but seeing the *Boston
Globe*s on the steps changed my mind. Then I didn't know
what to think. He was meticulous. Would've left me a note
if he'd gone away, and would have asked someone to pick
up the papers."

"What papers did you find? For which days?"

"Sunday's and Monday's."

"Not Saturday's? This is important."

"No. I didn't see a Saturday paper. I remember, because
the officer who talked to me when I reported Ray missing
asked the same thing," she said with conviction.

"What else did you notice?"

She continued: "I don't think any lights were on, but it was daytime . . . I might not have noticed. The front door was locked, the TV was off . . . I would have remembered if it wasn't." She paused. "There was one thing, though, really spooked me. I mentioned it to the other detective. The clock radio was blaring in the bedroom. It must have been on since six that morning."

"Did he set it every night? On weekends?"

"It's set so the radio turns on every morning at six o'clock. He has to remember to unset it on weekends, then on Sunday he turns it on again."

"What time on Sunday did he usually do this?"

"Whenever he thought of it. As long as it was after six A.M. it didn't matter." She shuddered remembering how frightening the music sounded in a house with no audience.

Dunn continued: "How about the kitchen?"

"It was clean. When he eats alone he rinses his dishes right away. Puts everything away. That detective checked the trash bag in the kitchen. . . . I don't know if he found anything."

"Mrs. Bishop, was anything missing from the house? Any sign he had packed for a trip, or that anything was stolen?"

"No. All his shaving stuff's here." She closed her eyes for a moment. When they opened again, she added: "No suitcases are gone."

"How about his wallet? Keys?"

"They . . . they're not here." She looked at him. "Weren't they with . . . on him?"

Dunn shook his head. He glanced around the kitchen. On the refrigerator door was a calendar advertising a local insurance company. He got up and walked over to it. The pages were held up by a pair of plastic pineapples and turned to March. On the side of the New England scene depicted above the rows of numbers was taped a neatly clipped Celtics regular season schedule from the *Boston Globe*. Dunn noticed a

few of the dates on the calendar had been circled, and assorted other annotations dotted the month.

"Mrs. Bishop, did your husband use this calendar?"

"Yes, we both did."

"Do you mind?" he asked as he lifted the page. She
shook her head. Dunn flipped to February and studied the
notes. Diagonal lines were drawn through February 6, 14,
and 22. Dunn asked about their meaning.

"Those were his days off. They change every week."

"Just one day a week?"

"Well, they always have Sundays off."

"What about the circles?" He had returned to March.

"I'm not sure," she answered. She looked up at the page
with little interest. "He was always circling days. All different reasons."

Dunn looked at her. The stones in her earrings picked up
the green in her eyes. He removed the pineapples and
brought the calendar over to the table. Starting with early
February and going to the end of March, he went through
each notation and asked her to translate.

Calendars were the same all over the world. They all had
hair and car appointments, undelivered papers, and visits to
the doctors. They all had color photos of local scenery and
small, discreet reminders of your need for insurance. Dunn
thought, what a lost opportunity for McHale Assurance. Why
bother with the covered bridge in the snow? Why not have
February's illustration be a red Mustang wrapped around a
telephone pole? Why not have March show a house burned to
the ground with only the refrigerator left standing? Standing
charred, its harvest-gold skin blackened and peeling, and
with two tiny pineapple magnets, now molten lumps, cling-
ing to the freezer door.

There were five remarks about missing *Globe*s during February and early March. None for Saturday, March 3, however. Most of the other notes she was able to illuminate,

with the exception of the word "Mackey" scribbled under Thursday, March 8.

"Yours, or his?" he asked.

"Must have been his. I don't recognize the name."

"You think definitely it's a name then?"

She raised an eyebrow. "What else would it be, Sergeant?"

He didn't answer. "Could I borrow this?"

She nodded.

Dunn stood up and thanked her for the coffee. "With your permission, Mrs. Bishop, I'd like to take a look at your husband's papers. Did he have a place where he kept correspondence? A file cabinet, or a desk?"

She led him to the dining room. On a sideboard was an enamel tray with what appeared to be current bills and a couple of letters. Opening the top drawer, she showed him where they kept a checkbook, bank statements, and the rest of the business end of their life. Dunn asked if he could take a few items back to the station.

"Whatever you want. Do whatever you want." She had held together pretty well, he thought. He stuffed them into a brown paper bag and prepared to leave. At the door, he turned and asked if anyone would be able to stay with her. She replied that her sister was on her way down from Gloucester.

"We may need you to make positive identification," he said. Considering the condition of the body, he planned on avoiding it if any male relatives were listed in the file. "If we do, you'll be contacted later on this afternoon to make arrangements. I will have to ask a few more questions, but they can wait till tomorrow."

"Why did he go to the train station?" she asked as he opened the front door.

"I don't know, Mrs. Bishop. But I intend to find out."

Small green stones. Claire's eyes had been blue.

Chapter 3

Sehet mich an: Ich habe eine kleine Zeit
Mühe und Arbeit gehabt.

Look upon me; for a little while
trouble and labor were mine.
—Ecclesiasticus 51:27

According to the file, the last person to have seen Ray
Bishop alive was the neighbor next door at No. 94. Walter
Pellegro lived with his nine-year-old daughter Annie at the
end of the road closest to the park. To the east and south he
was bounded by trees, to the west toward the center of town
lay Bishop's property. Separating the two yards was a six-
foot-high stockade fence stretching back halfway from the
sidewalk. This gave way to chain link the rest of the distance
to the rear property line.

Dunn looked at his watch. It was close to four. He deposited the bag on the seat of the Camaro and walked up Pellegro's front steps, taking a chance he would be home.

The man who opened the door was fair-haired, full-
bearded, tall, and muscular. Clutching half-opened mail in
one hand, he gave Dunn the impression he had only just
come home from work. On the floor behind him lay a hard

hat, a schoolbag, and a child's jacket. An attractive woman of about twenty-five stood in the living room and was in the process of removing her coat. When Dunn explained his purpose, the woman offered to leave.

"It's all right, Yvonne." He turned to Dunn. "Sergeant, this is a friend of mine."

Without further hesitation, Pellegro led the detective into the living room, pointed to a chair, and sat down across from him with a cooperative and attentive demeanor. Dunn brushed off some Doritos and took a seat.

"Mr. Pellegro, from your statement two weeks ago, you last saw Ray Bishop on Saturday the third of March. What time was that, and what did you see?"

"It was sometime between four and five in the afternoon. I had a couple friends over . . . we went out later. I went into the kitchen for refills, and happened to notice Ray getting into his car. His was the gray one, the Continental. He backed out of the driveway, turned toward town, and that's the last I saw of him."

"How can you be sure of the time?"

"Well, my friends came a little after three-thirty. We had sucked down one round of beers. The sitter showed up around five, so my best guess is four, four-thirty. I remember saying something to my buddies, like 'There he goes,' or something. They'd probably remember. They could back me up."

"I'm not suggesting you need 'backing up,' Mr. Pellegro. Was this before or after it started snowing, do you remember?"

"Right before, I think. I know it had started when we all left, but it wasn't snowing when I looked out the window. I'd have remembered if he brushed the car off."

"Was it parked in the driveway, or in the garage?" Dunn asked.

"Well, yeah, it was in the garage, I guess. He had to get

out to close the door. The fence back there is chain link. I could see pretty clearly.''

''And that's how you knew it was him? Was he alone?'' The man nodded.

''Where was Mrs. Bishop's car? It's a one-car garage, isn't it?'' Dunn continued.

''She wasn't around. At least her car wasn't. Her car's maroon. A Ford Escort. I don't remember seeing anyone around the rest of the weekend. I was gone part of the time.''

Dunn thought for a moment. ''Could you tell from where you were standing if there was anything unusual about him? Did he appear in a hurry . . . was he carrying anything?''

''No, not really. He could have put something in the car before I looked out. I didn't notice anything unusual.''

''What was he wearing?''

''Like I said two weeks ago, I don't remember. Except his jacket. Green winter jacket.''

''You said a sitter came . . . to stay with your daughter? Were they both here all Saturday night?''

''Yep. And Sunday. I went on a ski trip.''

''Tell me about the fence,'' Dunn said, remembering the earlier report.

Pellegro's voice grew quiet as he pulled on his beard. ''He said he put it up to keep his dog in. His dog was mostly spaniel. Not likely to jump six feet. And you'll notice along the front he's got a three-foot-high picket fence. So he didn't need it for the dog, did he? He made sure his view wasn't blocked. Mine sure was.''

''Was that the issue, your view?''

''Yeah. I looked into suing him, to make him take it down, but he wasn't breaking any laws. So there's nothing I can do about it.'' He smiled. ''Now he's gone, the dog's gone, but the fence is still here.''

Dunn stood up. He wanted to talk to the child.

''She's out in back,'' the woman volunteered. ''You won't

find her very friendly right now. She's been kind of upset."
She turned toward Pellegro. "Usually she's great with
strangers, isn't she, Walt?"

Pellegro nodded. He led Dunn into the kitchen and opened
the back door. Dunn looked over at the window and asked,
"Mr. Pellegro, what did you mean when you said to your
friends, 'There he goes'? What prompted that remark? Did
they know him?"

Pellegro was taken aback for a moment. "I must have
been talking to them about the fence."

Dunn swung open the storm door and stepped out into the
backyard. Ann Pellegro was sitting on the far swing, legs
dangling, shoulders slumped. He watched as both feet suddenly kicked back and forth, trying to tease the swing into
movement. Dunn smiled and walked toward the swing set.
Resisting the urge to give her a push, he settled himself in
the seat beside her.

"You must be Annie," he tried. The girl stopped kicking
and stared at the ground in front of her. Her flaxen hair
lifted in the offshore breeze. Sensing that no response was
forthcoming, Dunn got up, crouched in front of her, and
peered up into her face. Where normally such visual assault
would compel some acknowledgment, Dunn's eyes seemed
to repel the child's. Wherever he moved his face, she turned
to avoid it.

"She can't talk," her father called out from the back door.

"Is she deaf, Mr. Pellegro?" Dunn asked without turning.

"She's got some hearing loss . . . likes to crank up the
radio all the time. But she can hear your voice. She's retarded, though. She can't understand most of your words."

How retarded? Dunn wondered. He sensed a tension in
the child, but had no baseline to compare it to. Still, he
ventured, "Your friend said she was upset. Do you agree?"

Pellegro seemed to flush slightly: "Well, yeah, she has
been a little worked up the last couple weeks. I guess the

excitement and all. You know, the police coming by when he was missing and stuff. She picks up on things a lot— pretty sensitive. I'm keeping a closer eye on her, too, with a killer loose.''

Dunn stood up. If he were going to interview Annie Pellegro he would have to find a better way to reach her. This young girl with the serene round face appeared to spend a lot of hours in her backyard. She had a good view of the Bishops' dining-room windows, and through the chain link, of their yard as well. She had been home Saturday night, a crucial time period. Despite the partial deprivation of hearing, Dunn held out one small hope. People who didn't spend time talking often spent more time listening. And there didn't seem to be anything wrong with her eyes.

Dunn thanked the man, warned that he might have further questions, and handed him a card. Pellegro nodded. He ran his fingers through his hair and said he would do whatever he could to help.

Chapter 4

Siehe, ich sage euch ein Geheimnis.

Behold, I show you a mystery.
—1 Corinthians 15:51

Detective Jake Myles, who had a different Hawaiian shirt for every day of the week, had had primary responsibility in the missing-person investigation and Dunn now requested his help in the homicide. Myles had worked with him on many previous cases, and although he found his supervisor somewhat mediocre in the outfield, he felt Dunn to be more than competent on the job. Nevertheless, the two often worked in disharmony. In contrast to Myles's eager and impulsive manner, Dunn seemed to approach his work with a languidly orchestrated pace. Myles reluctantly tolerated their differences in tempo, but found Dunn's image to be an occasional disappointment. As an avid reader of crime fiction, Myles thought the guy played by too many rules. The purpose, after all, was to get the bad guys.

Wearing something with rows of brown lions, Myles caught up with Dunn at the station as the detective sergeant was returning from Monument Road. At his desk, Dunn filled the younger man in over styrofoam cups of burnt coffee, and they reviewed the remaining contents of the file. Dunn dug out a marker from his desk and labeled the bag of letters. Next he spread out the calendar and invited Myles to interpret the circles.

After about two minutes Myles broke into a wide grin. He grabbed the calendar and held it against his forehead. Closing his eyes and muttering for a moment, he then shouted: "Carnac says, the answer is Tuesday night!"

"Come on, Jake. Cut the crap."

Myles brought the calendar back down and pretended to rip it open like an envelope. "And the question was, 'When can I next catch Larry on Sportschannel?' "

Dunn looked extremely annoyed. Myles tossed the pages at him and said: "The answer is staring you in the face, sportsfan."

Dunn glared at him as he located March again. "I'll have you back directing parade traffic, pal." Bending down Dunn could see that, indeed, tomorrow's date was circled. Then he figured out, as Myles had, that Bishop had simply circled all dates which the Celtics schedule clipping listed as televised games. He looked up at Myles.

"The guy was careful," Myles said in a low voice.

Jesus Christ. Bishop probably labeled his tools, too.

"Is Mackey a basketball player?" Dunn asked, pointing to the March eighth entry.

"Bob Mackey? Football, I think."

Dunn scowled. He copied the name and date carefully onto a piece of scrap paper and handed it to Myles. "Find Mackey. Find out what he's doing on Bishop's calendar. Get your jacket. We're talking to a few more neighbors first. No, first lunch."

Myles looked at the clock. "It's nearly five. In my country we call this dinner."

"Is that your Monday shirt?" Dunn asked.

*   *   *

"We don't yet have a strong motive. Let's start with why the killer hid the body in the men's cottage," Dunn said as he and Myles were waiting at the McDonald's drive-thru speaker. A single burst of noise, lacking in both high and low frequencies and sounding like bacon frying, had promised, the pair guessed, to be with them in a second.

"He was buying time before anyone found the body?" Myles offered.

"Why not throw it in the undergrowth? Or the water?"

"Maybe the tide was going out and he couldn't risk waiting eight hours," Myles said. Most of Salem Willows was surrounded by mud flats and rocks, stretching nearly a hundred feet at low tide. Dragging a body over the rip-rap would have been difficult, even for a strong man. Except for the patch of sand on the small public beach, anywhere else one ventured into the water at low tide was sure to cost a shoe and win only aggravation. Dunn remembered braving the mud as a boy, looking for tide pools and beach glass. He could never walk barefoot or the shells would cut his feet. So summer after summer he offered up numerous pairs of foam-rubber thongs to the muck. But it was well worth it. If you were young and stood still for a few minutes, the mud would pull you in up to your Achilles' heels. Lest you doubted its animateness, the ground would spit at that moment, a few feet away. Then closer, then more frequently. Arms outstretched to steady yourself, you would suddenly shriek and try to withdraw. As tenacious as peanut butter, the mud would bar your extraction. You eventually worked your ankles and feet free with a succession of loud, sucking noises. But the thongs would remain behind.

"WelcometoMcDonald's, may Itakeyourorder?" They stared hard at the speaker. Eye contact is important when auditory cues are sabotaged.

"Two quarter-pounders with cheese, a large fries, and a

chocolate shake,'' Dunn, who was driving and therefore qualified to order, said loudly and slowly to the box.

"Anything to drink?'' came the cheerful reply. Dunn smiled at Myles. You can't fight programming.

"Just that shake,'' he replied, with matching enthusiasm.

The amount due was announced as if it were good news. They were given driving instructions, and moments later were rewarded with food.

Turning back onto Canal Street, Dunn said: "The end of the pier goes out beyond the mud, but it's probably lit at night. Too exposed. So's the beach, and the sand gives way to mud before water.''

"Anyway, wouldn't throwing him in the water only buy him a week or so? The sucker'd pop up after that. What about the bushes?''

Dunn replied: "The dogs would have turned him up the next day. Or the dirt bikers. Of course, the ground was frozen, so burying him would've been hard. No, I guess the cottage was a good choice, easy to get into, and with those rotting screw holes, he could push them back in and no one who came too close would suspect anything. At least until the weather warmed up. Course, we're assuming Bishop was killed in the park.''

He slurped at his shake. As the liquid receded, he wondered for a second if he would find a thong at the bottom. McDonald's shakes have gotten thinner, he thought. Back when they contained cholesterol they were so thick the straw was useless.

Myles watched him a moment, then replied: "Well, if he wasn't wasted in the park, why hide him there? The killer could have taken him to a lot better hiding places, places he fucking never would have come out of.''

Myles was right. The North Shore held many good dumping grounds, deep water included, for anyone willing to drive a few minutes with a bleeding corpse in the trunk. How, then, was Bishop lured to the park? Or did they meet by chance? Myles voiced a question which had been on Dunn's mind:

"You said the upper torso was clean but the rest of the body was dirty and covered with leaves. What's your explanation?"

"I think, judging by the pattern of the dirt, that the killer must have wrapped something around Bishop's head and shoulders while he was moving him. A jacket, or maybe a bag. Perhaps a trash bag."

"Why? Maybe to keep from getting blood on himself?"

"Makes sense," Dunn answered.

Myles swallowed the last piece of his quarter-pounder and fished around for the rest of the fries. He extended a small, twisted mass to Dunn, who declined. "How do you know the body was moved?"

Dunn answered: "There were no signs of a struggle inside the cottage. Most of the floor, which was pretty dirty, was undisturbed. A narrow section alongside the corpse looked like it had been wiped. Probably to obliterate footprints, though I think there were traces enough to make the lab happy. Also, we just agreed Bishop's head was wrapped so the killer could move him cleanly."

"How about if the bag was to blindfold him, he was led to the cottage, and they scuffled outside? That would explain the leaves and dirt on his pants." They were pulling up in front of 55 Monument Road, home to, among others, Mr. Dale Timothy Raider, plaintiff in last November's suit of *Raider versus Bishop.*

Dunn let the engine idle a minute before shutting it off. Then he said: "No, Bishop didn't hit the ground alive. At least he didn't push himself back up. His palms were clean."

Myles looked solemnly at the empty box in his hand. " 'Out, out brief candle,' " he muttered. Dunn wasn't sure if he was referring to Ray Bishop or the french fries.

                              *   *   *

They stepped out of the car and approached the house, which was on the cove side of the street. Number 55 stood out like the proverbial sore thumb when it came to yard work. Flanked on either side by lawns carefully mown in the fall before their winter's sleep, this yard was scruffy and still wore a good portion of October's leaves. Loose scraps of paper and a soda can were lodged among a row of untamed hedges. A pickup truck and a motorcycle inhabited the drive-way, as did the lid to a plastic trash can.

It was well into the visit before the members of the Raider household began to make any sense to Dunn, and even then, he wasn't sure "sense" was the word. Dunn and Myles were first greeted at the door by the dog. A bark like a cannon made them step back, despite the inch and a half of Stanley steel exterior door which separated them. Myles swore. After several rings, which struck Dunn as totally superfluous, the door was finally opened by a sturdy young teenager with a gash on the top of his head. The hair around the gash, which had been stitched, was shaved. The back of the boy's head sported a tail, however, so that Dunn couldn't be entirely sure whether the kid had an injury or a hairdo.

"Yeah?" the boy asked, one hand gripping the collar of a large Doberman-and-something-bigger mixed breed. The door was only half open in case the collar gave out.

"Sergeant Dunn, Detective Myles, Salem Police. We called earlier. Are you Mr. Raider?"

"Naw, that's my uncle. He's out in back. Ya wanna come in or go round back?"

"We'll go around." Dunn smiled at the dog, the door closed, and the two found their way to the backyard through some forsythias gone berserk. The lawn was not deep, ending in a sort of mangled sea wall at the edge of the water. At one end of the wall a makeshift dock jutted out at an angle, as if to avoid calling attention to itself. Tied to the dock was a small sailing dingy, and in the dingy was a man in his late thirties struggling with the mast. Squatting on the dock was a woman dressed in jeans and a blue plaid shirt, gesturing and explaining what was obviously, from the look on the man's face, unexplainable.

The detectives approached and introduced themselves. The woman was not Mrs. Raider, but she obviously lived there. On the porch overlooking the scene was another player, a young girl dressed in black, sitting on the swing and reading a book. She looked up and squinted at the two men. "Like we said on the phone, Mr. Raider, we're investigating the death of Ray Bishop. Could we go inside? We have a few questions."

The man climbed up onto the dock. He was Dunn's height, and sported the beginnings of a mustache. Wiping his hands off on his trousers, he led the way to the back door. Inside, the dog was shoved into a back room somewhere, where, much to Dunn's annoyance, it whined without stopping. Raider motioned for the two to sit down. The rest of the pack milled around close by, but at least they didn't whine.

"You knew Mr. Bishop?" Dunn began.

"No, not really. Only talked to him twice. I knew his dog."

"How?" asked Myles, who was taking notes.

"Dog came down every morning to crap on our front lawn. Your friend, Mr. Bishop, would stand a couple houses away, like he didn't notice. The minute the dog was done, Bishop would call him back. Then he'd turn and go back up the street."

"When did you first talk to him?"

"October. I remember 'cause the lawn was covered with leaves," Raider said. Dunn smiled to himself. With this yard it could just as well have been March. The man continued: "I saw the dog come down as I was looking out the front bedroom window. I was getting dressed for work. I also saw

Bishop, so I ran out the front door to the sidewalk just as the dog was finishing. I went over to the evidence and called out to him.''

"What happened?" Dunn asked.

"I said, 'Look what your dog did. Don't you think you should clean it up?' He denied it at first. I invited him down to examine it while it was still steaming. So he came down, but he was pretty pissed about it. Anyway, we started yelling at each other and then he started, well, threatening me with his fists. I didn't exactly say much to calm him. I was pretty mad. We go to a lot of trouble to keep our dog in our own yard. I have to clean up after him, why should I clean up after all the neighbors' goddamn dogs, too?''

"Did this convince him?"

"No. He swung at me. I ducked and then I pushed him. He fell down and then I helped him up. After he went home, I thought about it for a while and decided the asshole shouldn't get away with starting a fight. So I took him to court for assault.''

"The record shows the suit was dropped.''

"The day of the hearing we met with, I guess it was the clerk, to try and settle before going in front of the judge. He heard both our sides, chewed us both out, then suggested we drop it.''

"Why'd he chew you out?" Dunn asked.

"Only for letting the guy get to me. I shoulda backed off. But he lectured him about cleaning up after his dog, how antisocial it is when you don't, and also reminded him Salem has a leash law. He also warned him about trying to settle arguments with his fists. That's when Bishop fucked up.''

Dunn leaned forward. Myles looked up from his pad.

"He told the clerk he'd been in hundreds of fights before, and no one had been ass enough to take him to court!'' Raider said incredulously. Dunn and Myles looked at each other. Had Bishop found one last challenger two weeks ago?

"Did he mend his ways after that?" Myles asked.

"Seems to have. Haven't even seen the dog in a couple months, have we?" he asked the rest of the household. They shook their assorted heads. The policemen left a card and took their leave.

As they climbed into the Camaro, Dunn scribbled down the plate numbers in the driveway. "Let's run these," he said.

Chapter 5

Dies irae

Day of wrath
—Requiem "Dies irae"

It was getting late. Dunn turned the car back toward the park. Directly behind the concession line was an enclave of houses known as Juniper Point. The sociology of the neighborhood differed sharply from the Monument Road neighborhood, separated by park, woods, and military service. Monument Road homes faced the sheltering lee of Collins Cove, enjoying dry basements and neatly trimmed, modestly spacious lawns. Juniper Point houses faced directly onto Salem Sound and the Atlantic Ocean. Despite their precarious and vulnerable state, homes on the Point huddled defiantly together in quixotic eccentricity. Behind the arcade were the artists, the Willows activists, the wine tasters, cedar shingles, and cluttered alleyways to the water's edge. In a world of their own, nevertheless situated on the periphery of the park, they enjoyed a proximity to the cottages that could prove fortuitous. The two men split up to canvas those houses immediately adjoining the park, in particular the ones with views of the men's cottage.

No one had seen anything suspicious the weekend of the

third. They had noticed a few dedicated joggers, the usual year-round strollers, but not much else. Certainly no forced break-ins to the men's room. A few had heard or known of the Bishops, although by and large the two neighborhoods kept to themselves. One woman, however, who regularly distributed leaflets and organized functions for local causes had been aware that the Bishops were not getting along.

"It seems whenever I came to the door he'd be yelling at the top of his lungs. Not the most friendly guy. Did you hear about the windshield?"

Dunn indicated that he hadn't.

"Last Labor Day. Pretty crowded down here at the Willows. Lots of people picnic here every Labor Day. All the streets get parked up. Anyway, someone was down here selling souvenir gulls made out of marble or something. They were pretty solid, and heavy, not something you'd lug around all day at a picnic. But a lot of the neighbors were buying them. I got one myself. They were beautiful. So Ray Bishop buys one for his wife. When he walks home he finds someone illegally parked in his driveway. Does he call the police? Does he call a tow truck? No! He wigs out. In front of half the neighborhood he smashes the windshield in with his wife's marble gull."

The woman's face retained a dramatic expression as she led him to the door. He thanked her, and she answered him with a satisfied smile.

While waiting for Myles to return to the car, Dunn decided to take another look around the park itself before the sun disappeared. He began to walk the perimeter, looking for scars of a scuffle on the ground that might, with the season's isolating influence, have been preserved. He knew the police had combed this ground already. He also knew what he was really searching for was a motive.

He checked the pier. The water looked deep enough on one side, probably dredged for the tour boat which docked there during the summer. There was indeed a light at the end, already glowing in the dusk. Out in the sound, Great Misery Island was crawling under the night sky to the east.

Stretching south from the pier was a public beach. Small and gray, its mussel shells and tiny rocks were deposited by the tide in long rows, giving it a look more industrial than recreational. Less evocative of a Bermuda sandy shoal, it was instead reminiscent of a wire fence, barnacles biting the feet like barbs. The dim illumination from the end of the pier cast artificial shadows on the dark sand like a prison searchlight.

Dunn turned back. Leaving the pier he noticed a sign on the bait house at its entrance, which invited fishermen to feed the lobsters and one below which implored No Dumping. *Well, that explains why the body wasn't here.* He smiled to himself. He didn't see any lobsters.

The harbor waters to the north began picking out isolated lights from the few masts of boats not stored for the winter. Through the willow trees he could look westward along the shore into the cove where the sun had nearly set. Taking the long way back to the car, he traced the rocky shoreline that led that way. Two gulls broke into a cacophony of shrieks and cries over a piece of garbage on the stones below him. Dunn rounded a bend. The trees were behind him and continuous open sky stretched from the horizon beyond the cove to far above his head—more sky than people are used to who live in cities or among trees and power lines. And the expanse of sky was on fire, with cloud formations that for a few amazing seconds ignited in deep and angry reds. For a moment they intensified, then slowly subsided as he watched, glowing embers subtly graying until they no longer glowed and one could no longer recall their anger. A silent, visual climax to Bishop's day of wrath.

Chapter 6

Confutatis maledictis,
flammis acribus addictis.

*The damned are silenced
and doomed to painful flames . . .*
    —Requiem "Dies irae"

Despite the coldness of the March night, Thomas Weber woke up at three-thirty in the morning drenched with sweat. The night had been a loss. His ears still rang with the sound of gunfire, heart still pounded from the running. But it was the violent shaking that awakened him, for at that moment his pursuers had caught up with him. He sat upright and stared into the dark, trying to focus his eyes on some object, any real object to wrench himself out of the past, both distant and recent, and into the present. *It's OK, it's OK*, he said over and over to himself. But it was not entirely OK.

The coffee maker erupted in a violent, noisy burst of steam, signaling that the brewing was complete. After a few final sputters Lila Weber gingerly pulled out the carafe and filled two waiting mugs. She carried them over to the break-fast table and slid into the seat across from her husband. Tuesday's *Boston Globe* was gazing up at him unopened, but he was not returning the look. Weber helped himself to the sugar bowl, shoveled in two heaping spoonfuls, then began to stir. "We're out of cream," his wife apologized. He said nothing and continued to stir, long after even the most stubborn of lumps would have dissolved.

"It may be time to move," he said.

Her mug was halfway to her lips when her hands started to shake.

"Not again," she said, shocked and dismayed. Coffee spilled out onto her wrist. She set the mug down and grabbed for a dish towel to stop the burning. "What happened?"

"A man was found murdered yesterday down at the Willows. They were talking about it at the White Hen last night when I went in for the bread. I knew the guy. We were together in Korea."

"Oh, God," she said, stunned. After a pause, she asked: "Who? Was he from here? Did he know you were here?"

"A guy named Bishop. A mailman, for chrissake. I don't think he was our usual carrier. He might have been filling in . . . came by the last Saturday in February. I waited for him to go back down the walk and out of sight before I opened the door to get the mail, but then suddenly he turned around and came back . . . forgot to leave the *TV Guide*. So there we were, face-to-face. It's been probably thirty-eight years, Lila, but we both recognized each other immediately. Took me a moment to place him, and I'm not sure he realized then where he knew me from, but eventually it came to him."

"How do you know?"

"Because four days later I got a letter. He must have jotted down our name from the *TV Guide*."

"What did it say?" She could barely speak.

Weber stood up and looked out the kitchen window. They had shared this small backyard with their landlord for the past nine years, each year daring to plant a bit more than the previous season. Weber turned the flower beds every spring with caution, lest he call God's attention to himself, risking wrath and exposure. Last fall Lila had decided to stick a few bulbs into the ground beneath the kitchen window, where the March sun would reach into the late afternoon. In Lila's mind the flowers were not flags of betrayal but offerings of appeasement, tendered to win another year of God's coconspiracy.

A couple of green shoots were starting to push up. Weber suspected now that they would never see them bloom. His heart began to ache.

"The letter said that he knew about me, but that the secret was safe. He wanted one payment and would never bother us again." His voice turned sarcastic and bitter. "One small payment. At the end it said I would be contacted in a few days, when I had gotten the money together. He wanted two thousand dollars."

"What did you do?" she asked, shocked.

"I got a cash advance on our credit card. We didn't have that much in our account. Then I got a call from him the next weekend. You were at Leona's. Helping her with inventory. I think he was disguising his voice, but he told me to bring the cash to Forest River Park. So I did."

"Why didn't you tell me? Why did you pay him?"

"I didn't want to upset you just yet, and I wanted to buy time. You were finishing up with Leona, and you were about to get your bonus at the store."

"It was nowhere near two thousand dollars!"

"Come on," he said. "It was worth a lot more to you."

She sat back down, towel still around her wrist, and said softly, "But he's dead now."

"He may have told someone. He may have left something in writing. If he did, the police will come around. And if they do, sooner or later they'll find out."

Lila Weber looked around her kitchen. They had managed

to stay in Salem nearly ten years. In the early days of their marriage they had moved frequently, out of nervousness. "I'm sorry," he said after a while. She managed a half-smile. She hadn't chosen this life on the run, this life with no close friends, no deep roots, no real identity. But she had chosen this man.

At seven-thirty the same Tuesday morning, Dunn arrived at the station to hunt up Jake Myles. Together they drove to the Salem post office to talk to Bishop's fellow letter carriers before they set out on their routes. They split up, Dunn to the postmaster's office, Myles to talk to the co-workers. Many had known the victim for years, but not all had liked him. Most felt Bishop was reliable, stubborn, friendly until you crossed him. Some attributed his temper to his war days, but others felt that Ray Bishop was simply a fighter by nature.

The postmaster, Mrs. Nevins, was a black woman in her late forties, who refused to be referred to as "postmistress." Dunn remembered with amusement the last female postmaster he had met. She had done over the entire substation office, infusing it with her personality and homey touch. The small lobby and counter had been painted pink, and art works on consignment lined the walls wherever the usual post office posters had left gaps. Salem's post office, however, looked precisely like a post office. Behind Mrs. Nevins's oak door, the room was businesslike and austere, with the exception of some office shrubbery.

Dunn asked about Bishop's schedule just prior to his disappearance. The postmaster went down to the supervisor's office and brought back the schedule book.

"Mrs. Nevins, according to his wife, Bishop was off Saturday the third. Is that correct?" Dunn asked the woman. The single large window was filled with plants. The low morning sun cast a green glow on the carpet.

The postmaster opened the book, flipped through the pages, and said finally: "That's right, he had that Saturday off. And the Friday before."

"And Sunday?"

"Every six weeks they get Friday, Saturday, and Sunday off." She looked back down at the book. "The week before, his days off were Thursday and Sunday."

Dunn glanced down at his notebook. That agreed with the Bishops' calendar.

"Did Bishop ever have any problems with anyone on his route that you know of? Residents he might have had a fight with? Didn't get along with? I guess at his age he must have been pretty acquainted with his, whatever you call them, patrons?"

"Well, actually, he changed routes a couple of months ago. But no, I haven't heard of any problems. I'll check with the supervisor, though, and get back to you. He'd be more likely to know."

"Why'd he change routes? So close to retirement."

"The route off Highland Avenue became vacant. It's the only mounted route in Salem. Includes parts of Gallows Hill, Witchcraft Heights. Lots of condos and apartment complexes. You're in the jeep a lot of the time. An attractive route for an older carrier. Less walking."

"Where was his old route?" the detective asked.

"In North Salem."

Dunn, who lived in North Salem himself, looked startled. Maybe he had been on Bishop's route. Maybe that's why his mail had taken a recent downturn. No letters, no checks. Just bills and ads. Bills and ads didn't need a postman. They walked to your door by themselves.

Dunn thanked her and turned to leave. Mrs. Nevins looked up abruptly. "Sergeant Dunn . . . you said your name was 'Gabe?' Is that for 'Gabriel?' " The detective looked at her and nodded. She gave him a warm smile.

"Gabriel. The messenger. Patron saint of postmen. Good luck in your case, Sergeant."

Dunn rejoined Myles. They compared notes on the way back to the station. Myles negotiated the unmarked Crown Victoria around Riley Plaza with one hand and lit a cigarette with the other. Dunn rolled down the window.

"Listen, Jake, I'm going to find out where Annie Pellegro goes to school. Her teacher could shed some light on what she's capable of picking up on. I really believe she saw something that weekend. I just need to figure out how to talk to her."

He nodded toward the courthouse, a few blocks up the street from the plaza. "When you get a chance, why don't you go up and check for records of any other lawsuits against or by Ray Bishop. We still need a motive, Jake."

"You got a docket or date for me? Otherwise, forget it. There's enough bound volumes up there to fill the armory."

"Stick to the past year, then." That much was on computer.

Myles looked resigned. "So you think maybe the killer tried some other more legal avenue of retribution first?"

"Distinct possibility. Also, let's find out what happened to the Bishops' dog. That neighbor Raider said he hadn't seen it for months. Mr. Pellegro mentioned it, too, come to think of it. You can start with the dog constable, then try the local veterinarians."

Back at their desks, Myles began checking on the dog. Dunn pulled out the Bishops' calendar and glanced at his watch. It was quarter to nine, a decent enough hour. He called Coleen Bishop to remind her she had a hair appointment at one-thirty in the afternoon.

"I'll try to get your things back to you sometime later today, Mrs. Bishop," he added.

Chapter 7

Et misericordia ejus
a progenie in progenies
timentibus eum.

And the fearful shall be pitied,
from generation to generation.
—Luke 1:50

The Reading School was actually located in North Reading, some twelve miles northwest of Salem. Affiliated with a local college, it provided day programs for multi-handicapped children, including many from institutions in the area. As the principal led him down a dingy beige corridor toward the classrooms, Dunn thought that the place had all the cheerfulness of a VA hospital. The hallway was uncomfortably reminiscent of the wing of his own elementary school where the "resource room" and special education services classroom were located. His own childhood had given him more than a passing acquaintance with special ed teachers. The sight of colored construction paper shapes on each door rekindled in him old fears, fears of failure and exclusion.

Outside some of the classrooms were parked wheelchairs in assorted sizes and colors. Bags and knapsacks hung from the backs, and occasional trays of plastic or wood rested on the arms or leaned against the wall. They stopped at a door with a frosted window decorated with the names of the six occupants: WELCOME Tony, Karen, Chris, Fernando, Michael, Annie! The principal swung open the door, and Dunn found himself confronted with a room which could only be described as making the best of difficult circumstances. Brown plastic milk crates were stacked beside the door and served as cubbies for lunchboxes and changes of clothes. Makeshift hooks lined the wall on the right for jackets and bags. Toys and books, shabby and uninviting, were stacked on the windowsill with a jar of peanut butter and several boxes of crackers. A yellowed plastic pitcher that once must have been white rested on a low table, surrounded by plastic cups with lids and spouts.

The children were gathering around a large table for snacktime. Three in wheelchairs were pushed up and braked. Trays were being clamped into place, and an aide took one of the remaining kids out the door to fetch water. A young boy with a mop of curly hair was stretched out, relaxed and limp, on a mat in the corner with what Dunn guessed to be a physical therapist kneeling beside him. At that moment the teacher, a fair-haired woman named Mel Isaksen, excused herself to retrieve the boy's chair from the hall. When she returned with it and had set the brakes, the therapist carefully curled the boy up and positioned him in the chair. Once he was tightly buckled, she released him. The boy's limbs stiffened and his head was thrown back. The teacher wheeled him up to the table and turned around to face the policeman. The principal introduced them and left.

She gave him a broad, full-lipped smile. "Please call me Mel. We all use first names here. You're here to see Annie?"

"Mainly to observe. We met last night. I want to know how to reach her. I think she has something to tell me."

"Why don't you join us? Would you like some juice?

My aide went for water and is bringing Annie back from occupational therapy on the way.''

Dunn declined the juice, and selected a seat by the window. Not that he was squeamish, but the sight of forty wet fingers undulating around the table made him queasy. Four pairs of eyes were fixed on him now, and a couple of grins which terrified him. He felt that his discomfort was probably the only handicap in the room for which there was no accommodation.

A moment later Annie came in with the aide, the pitcher of water, and Chris, deducing from the empty, personalized place mats. If Annie recognized him, she didn't show it. The teacher greeted her with a combination of some sort of sign language and speech—"Annie, what did you do in OT?"— all the while getting the kids fixed up with crackers and apple juice. The therapist offered to stay and help with snacktime, since the classroom was apparently short a staff member.

Annie said nothing. "You tied something today, didn't you? What did you tie?" The girl brought her fists together in a sign, and the teacher responded: "Shoes? Great! Shoes!" Annie pursed her lips, attempting the word.

Resource Room was never like this.

Mel brought over a tray of peanut butter and crackers to Dunn. "She's been unusually quiet recently. She has some speech, but is far better in sign."

"How much can she understand?" Dunn inquired, graciously declining the snack.

"Quite a bit. I'd say, between a two- and three-year level of comprehension." To Dunn's surprised look, she added: "That's more than people think. Expressive language is less, though. She has some two-word sentences, a vocabulary of a couple hundred signs or so."

"Can you tell me if there have been any recent changes in her behavior?"

Mel suggested they step into the hall, assuring her aide they would only be a minute.

"Sergeant, could I ask what this is about? Does it have anything to do with her home environment? I thought Department of Social Services usually . . ."

"No, no. I guess I didn't make myself clear to your principal. I'm investigating a homicide in Salem. I have a suspicion that Annie might have witnessed something. I need your help in finding out."

She looked puzzled, then slightly horrified. "My God. No wonder she's upset."

"How do you mean?"

"She's been acting out quite a bit the last week or two. Like this morning, for example, I was playing a tape she really likes, and she started to throw things. Annie is never like that."

"What tape?"

"Oh, what was it . . . a Peter Gabriel album, his first one." Voices within were sounding at the rapidly thinning edge of control. "I'm going to have to go back in," she said, apologetically.

Dunn took her address and phone number and asked if he could stop by her home after work. She lived on the North Shore, not far from Salem. "Fine," she said, and slipped back inside. As the door swung shut, Dunn stared at the names in six bright colors which now faced him again, taunted him, daring him to reenter, to learn what he had come to learn, but their bold capital letters knew he would not, knew that he would flee to the world of the physically whole.

Cabot Street Antiques, located on the outskirts of Beverly, had gradually lost some of its identity over the years. No longer just antiques, used furniture, and bric-a-brac, it now sold new furniture in unfinished pine, not-so-local arts and crafts, maple sugar candy from Vermont, rented videotapes, and sported a small lunchroom. Earlier in the winter Dover had taken a job at the store after leaving her home and similar position in Ossipee, New Hampshire. Although her room downtown was still alien and temporary, Dover fit into the job as though it were home.

Dover had spent the morning pricing used books in the basement, then had gone upstairs to help with lunch. The radio in the kitchen was playing a Tom Petty song. Dover set about peeling eggs. Turning at the sound of the swinging door behind her, she gave a smile of recognition to Gene Bettencourt, who pumped gas across the street, and who came over for lunch and the company whenever he could. At twenty-one, he was two years younger than Dover.

"So when are you going to see him?" Gene asked, drawing up a stool.

"Dunno," she said quietly. She was beginning to regret having confided in him. "Soon. Maybe this Sunday."

"You need help?"

"Nope."

"What if he won't see you? What if he's . . . not nice? You don't know what you're walking into, Dover."

"I'll be all right."

He watched her smash the next egg against the hard surface of the table, possibly the only genuine antique in the building, he was fond of informing her. Deftly she turned it over and over, until the loud smacks subsided into soft noises as crazed as its shell had become.

"You've had the damn address for almost a month," he said, and stood back up. "Can I get a Coke?"

She nodded. The next egg was one of those where the shell doesn't come off but the white does. She swore as she had to scrape chunks off each bit of shell. For egg salad it didn't matter much, but it slowed her down.

"I've been busy. Payroll taxes last week, seasonal inventory orders this week."

"Just excuses, Dover," he said, mocking her. "What will it take you, one hour?"

"I don't know what it'll take." There was something between tiredness and fear in her voice. No, not fear; she couldn't be afraid. The hard part was over. One thing left to do. And Gene was right. It only needed an hour. After three years, only one hour. Why, then, was she dragging her heels?

"You want company?" he asked, trying another tack.

"Thanks, Gene, but no." Dover finally granted him a look.

She slipped the last egg out of its crumbled shell and began laying them one at a time in the egg slicer. A quick press, then quickly rotate the egg before it confronts the fact it's no longer whole, then a second press. "That's so neat," Gene said in wonderment.

Dover thought that the two years she had on the younger man must be important ones.

Chapter 8

Selig sind, die da Leid tragen,
denn sie sollen getröstet werden.
Die mit Tränen säen, werden mit Freuden ernten.

Blessed are they that mourn,
for they shall have comfort.
They that sow in tears shall reap in joy.
                    —Matthew 5:4, Psalm 126:5

"Walt?" The woman's voice was strident. Pellegro shifted the receiver and lowered his voice.

"Faith . . . I'm working right now. I'm talking to a customer."

"Oh, I thought you'd be having lunch now. I haven't heard from you in a couple weeks. You OK?"

"Yeah, I'm fine." Sounding slightly guilty, he added: "Thanks for the ride that night."

"No problem. Your skis are still here, y'know. Did you ever get your car?"

"Yep. They ripped me off. They always do. I hate mechanics. Listen . . . I'll pick up the skis later. I won't need them for a while."

"OK. Well, anyway, I . . . enjoyed that Sunday night. We gonna do it again sometime?" she asked.

"Right. I'll call you. This guy's waiting, Faith." He hung up. Why the hell couldn't Yvonne have been home that night?

It was lunchtime Tuesday when Dunn returned from Reading and stopped at the station for Myles. He wanted to talk to Mrs. Bishop again before her hair appointment and his autopsy at two o'clock. Myles shared a bologna sandwich with him in the car. "I didn't know you could cook," Dunn said appreciatively.

Mrs. Bishop answered their knock almost immediately, and led them to the front room. Originally it must have been a porch, but was now fully enclosed and weather-tight. Motioning to a pair of olive-green Naugahyde chairs, she offered them some coffee. Dunn handed her the calendar and the bulk of the letters he had borrowed. She took them with her to the kitchen. The men waited for her to reappear with the cups before sitting down. When she had perched nervously on the edge of one chair, Dunn turned to face her in the other. Myles settled himself on the couch but did not take out a notebook.

"Mrs. Bishop, what was your husband like?" Dunn asked gently. "What sort of life did you have together?"

There was a long silence. Finally: "My husband was not always easy to get along with," she said carefully. "He was not a mean man, but he had a temper. He liked to have his way."

"How did you meet him?" Dunn asked.

"I work for the insurance agency that handled his property insurance. Ray came in one day about six years ago, to sign some papers in connection with a claim. His first wife had passed away, and he just seemed terribly lonely. Anyway, we got to talking in the outer office while he was waiting for the agent. Finally he went in, but when he was through, he stopped by my desk again and invited me out for coffee."

"What was the claim about?" Dunn inquired.

"There had been some damage from a fire—I think it was sparks from his fireplace or something. It wasn't extensive—smoke damage and part of the floor needed replacing. And a couch. I wasn't there, of course."

"And that was six years ago?"

"Yes. We started seeing each other. He seemed nice—seemed to care about me. He wasn't just looking for company. And I guess I was about ready to settle down."

Dunn hid his surprise. She must have been in her mid- to late thirties at the time, a secretary in a small agency. *Wild* was not a word that came to mind. He nodded. "So you married and moved into his house, here?"

"The question of going somewhere else never came up. I had a small apartment off Bridge Street, which was obviously unsuitable. He'd had this place built in the fifties. After seeing how much he had put into it, I didn't have the heart to ask him to move."

"But you considered it?"

"There's nothing wrong with the house. It has a wonderful view, a nice neighborhood, close to work . . ." Her voice trailed off.

"Ghosts?" he offered.

She paused. "Yes." She gestured towards the walls. "He wouldn't let me change the color of the paint, even when it needed a new coat. The kitchen was *hers*, and still is, after six years."

She stopped. Dunn thought, ironically, that it was Coleen Bishop's kitchen now.

She went on to describe their years together, how more and more she felt compared to the first Mrs. Bishop, and suffering in the comparison. Despite his quick temper, he never showed physical violence toward her. But she never won his approval, either.

"Did you ever tell him how you felt?"

"What would have been the point? I really don't like getting into arguments. He'd just bury his head in the paper, or
the TV or the cereal box. But maybe I should have been
more insistent." She started to cry. Tears of inadequacy and
anger, mourning not her bereavement, not the eternity of his
death, but the six years of her life with him.

Dunn just listened. Coleen Bishop had two ghosts to exor-
cise. After a while he asked: "What happened to the dog?"

"Muffet?" She looked surprised. "She died last year."

"Wasn't she young? The dog officer said she was three
or four."

"She was hit by a car," Mrs. Bishop said without looking up.

Somehow Dunn didn't think so. "Mrs. Bishop, did your
husband ever strike the dog? Maybe the dog gave him reason
to be angry and he lost control? Hit her harder than he meant
to?" When she remained silent, he added softly: "He's dead
now. You don't need to protect him."

She spoke very quietly. "He told me she was run over. I
wasn't here, and he didn't talk about it much." Her eyes,
however, seemed to tell another story, seemed to confirm his
suspicion.

"You must have been very fond of the dog." Three
ghosts, he thought. And in the response on her face he wondered if he saw a motive.

> Salve me, fons pietatis.
> *Save me, O spring of mercy.*
> —Requiem "Rex tremendae"

Four days before reporting her husband missing, Coleen
Bishop had opened her small blue book and turned to the
appropriate page for March 1:

" . . . *there can be no progress without humility.*"

With no small degree of skepticism, she read then that she
must surrender to God's will as the only way of escaping

both the destructive life to which she had meekly submitted
and the distress she caused herself in the erroneous pursuit
of self-will.

Coleen closed the book again and slipped it between the
mattresses. Ray knew she attended Al-Anon, but she couldn't
bear him flipping through the pages and mocking its contents.
Surrendering to the program was difficult enough. She remained seated on the edge of the bed for several minutes,
staring at the braided rug in soft reds and grays at her feet.
A dimple had formed in the middle, which maddeningly refused to be pushed flat. If God's will was not defined as the
hand she was dealt, nor was it defined as the cards she would
throw back, then how the hell was it defined? For five minutes she humbled herself.

*The attitude of true humility confers dignity and grace on
us, and strengthens us to take intelligent spiritual action in
solving our problems,* it had continued under March 1.

Ray had finished his fourth beer and was watching a basketball game in the living room. They had consumed a joy-
less dinner of undercurried curry, and had discussed whether
it would be a good idea to drive up to New Hampshire for
the weekend. Coleen liked going up in the off season and
walking through the snowy woods. The year-round motel on
Route 16 had a spectacular view of the mountains. But Ray
had thought it was a bad idea and dropped the subject. Anyway, there was a game Saturday.

Coleen stood up and looked at herself in the mirror. Even
with effort she could muster no grace, no dignity. Her face
said simply, "I've made a mistake." Answers still declined
to rain down upon her. The will of God refused to reveal
itself. Finally she moved to the closet and hauled out a small
vinyl suitcase. She planned to stay with her sister for a few
days, if not to change her hand, at least to examine it.

As she bent down to fish her running shoes from under
the bed, her hand fell upon Muffet's vinyl squeaky crab,

now dry and silent. She pulled it out for a moment, then replaced it and started packing. When you lose your dog, you lose your most loyal fan. She had finished crying for Muffet, however. She cried now only for herself.

Now she must tell Ray, and must with all her determination keep him from stopping her, from talking her out of going. Composing her speech in careful words, Coleen walked resolutely into the living room and stood behind her husband's chair.

"Ray?" She always started difficult conversations this way. "Ray?"

"What?" he answered without turning. The *t* was heavily aspirated with the suggestion of annoyance.

"Ray, I was thinking that I'd like to go spend some time with Angela . . ."

"Go ahead."

". . . because I feel I need . . ." She realized then that he had ended the argument before it began. His words were not a blessing but a dare. He wouldn't stop her now, but his anger would be unbearable when she came back. Coleen would leave in fear and return in dread.

Returning to the bedroom for the suitcase, Bishop's wife took a quick, automatic look around, turned off the light, and headed back down the hall to the front door. When you're being watched not by eyes but by the back of a head, walking becomes suddenly an unlearned skill. She was conscious of even the sound of her footsteps, trying not to move too fast lest she appear to be bolting, but not too slowly, lest she appear to be tiptoeing. Holding her breath to disclose neither the fear nor the eagerness, she held a nonchalant pace up to the end of the hall and opened the door measuredly. Daring one last glance, she could see him in the living room. Just then he turned to look at her and the hair rose on the back of her neck. Mustering up all her courage, she met his eyes for a moment then stepped out into the darkness.

When the car reached Webb Street Coleen began to shiver. Turning the corner, she pulled over to the curb and waited until the violent shaking in her hands subsided. She forced herself to think about the best route to Gloucester this time of night, and of her sister, and whether she should call. She was at last able to continue, and it was several blocks before she thought of Eric. Should she call him? Easier from the highway than from Angela's.

Just as she hit Route 128 it started to pour. Eric will wait till morning, she thought. I'm enough for me to handle right now. I can't handle him as well.

Chapter 9

Agnus dei, qui tollis peccata mundi,
dona eis requiem.

Lamb of God, who lifts away the sins of the world,
give them rest.

—John 1:29

The sound of a buzz saw ripping through skull is like no other. Dr. Mei had completed the external exam and was attacking the head. As she worked she dictated her findings into a cassette recorder by her side. The saw seemed to intensify the smell. Dunn took and held another breath. The photographer from CPAC backed away to reload his camera. Deep inside the ceiling vent a fan rattled ineffectually, and Dr. Mei's assistant sprayed air freshener high over the table.

"Cause of death looks like blunt trauma, mechanism most likely subcranial hemorrhage." Dr. Mei had removed the skull and appeared to be reading the surface of the brain. "Skull fracture, associated subdural hematoma." She switched off the recorder and glanced at Dunn. "The dilation of the right pupil tells us he was alive when hit."

The witnesses watched with momentary solemnity as she lifted and weighed the brain. Inspired by the familiarity of the white enamel scale, the photographer embarked upon a steady stream of predictable butcher-shop jokes. Humor in the autopsy room, just as at the scenes, was horrible and tasteless. Yet it was a necessary part of the distancing. Of keeping death away. Of giving oneself permission to go about the job unencumbered.

"You're a sick man," Dr. Mei said to the photographer.

Starting with a Y-shaped incision, the medical examiner opened up the torso and gave Bishop a physical few know in their lifetimes. Every organ was weighed and described. Except for liver findings consistent with the onset of cirrhosis, the man had been in reasonable health. Dunn watched with interest as she removed the stomach contents and bagged them for the lab. Next to the skull, Bishop's last meal was Dunn's most reliable witness. He looked at the doctor with raised eyebrows.

"Well, from the looks of it, I'd guess he died less than two hours after eating. I'll try to get an analysis for you by the end of the week," she said. Anticipating his next question, she added: "The settling of the blood doesn't support the position you found him in. I would have to say he was moved during the first hour or so. And the wound would have bled considerably more than you saw in there. Find the puddle, Gabriel, and you'll find your killer."

"Thanks, Mom. You make a fine detective. How about a quick blood alcohol?" The complete toxicology would take a couple of weeks to come back from Boston. To the crime lab, Salem's Biggest Case was an oxymoron.

Dr. Mei nodded to the assistant who had set down the can of Glade to prepare sample vials for the lab. The doctor peeled off her gloves and switched back on the recorder. " 'It is the opinion of the undersigned, blah, blah, pending toxicology. The manner . . .' " She switched it off. "What is it, boys? Any doubts?"

The CPAC photographer raised his hand. "Clearly suicide."

Dunn smiled at Gloria.

'' 'The manner will be listed as homicide.' ''

The medical examiner turned on the Smith Corona at the end of the counter and began filling out the death certificate. Dunn looked over at the remains on the steel table, the sound of water still running somewhere below the mesh surface. Like a babbling mountain brook. No, not like a babbling brook. The forest-scented Glade was getting to him.

A good chunk of Dunn's overtime outside of court was spent in this room. The CID investigated most unattended deaths in Salem. Any suspicious ones were posted. Whoever was on duty and caught the call also attended the autopsy. In Dunn's opinion, most of the answers to each murder were spread out on this table. Maybe in a hundred years they would know all the questions. Maybe the next technological breakthrough would allow them to see the murderer's face burned into the optic nerve, or to measure the killer's desperation on the skin of the victim the way they do powder burns. But today this corpse was nearly done talking. *Rest in peace, pal*, Dunn said silently.

The assistant took a few more minutes to type the blood and determine the BAC. She looked up from the microscope. "Type's AB."

Dunn smiled. He loved rare blood.

"He blew a one-three," she announced finally, as if she were going to book him.

The photographer turned to the corpse. "Mr. Bishop, are you on any medications?"

Dr. Mei looked at Dunn. "Sounds like he had had a few. Consistent with the liver involvement. Is that any help?"

Dunn frowned. "I don't know yet. What about the weapon? And do you think his death was instantaneous?"

The state photographer was not giving up. "Are you contemplating, or have you contemplated suicide, Mr. Bishop?" The assistant laughed.

Dr. Mei ignored them. "By the skull damage it looked

like he was hit once from in front with a cornered object. Smooth textured, hard enough not to fragment. Your perpetrator was probably right-handed, but that's your department. I found no vomiting, no bite marks in the mouth, or other evidence of seizures. Minimal clotting. I'd say, yes, it was sudden. He was lucky. Clean and swift. We should be able to release the body tomorrow.''

Clean and swift. His hangover would have been worse.

From Salem Hospital, Dunn stopped home to shower and change. It was nearly four when he returned to the station. Myles was down at the front desk running names and numbers through the computer. Upstairs Dunn dug the phone out from the afternoon pile of notes that had drifted onto his desk and called Mrs. Bishop's sister to arrange a visit. Then he rang downstairs and asked for his partner. ''Jake, I'm starving. I owe you lunch . . . Fine. Call it whatever you want. Let's go.'' Myles agreed to meet him at the car.

As Dunn stepped out the front door of the station, he caught sight of Brian Hurd climbing out of his cruiser. The detective gave a quick wave as he passed. He remembered then that Hurd kept an extensive tape collection in his locker, a collection that put Strawberries Records to shame. He turned and asked: ''Brian, any chance you have Peter Gabriel in your locker? First album?''

''Mmh'' came Hurd's squeaky reply. ''I'll check. I'll leave it on your desk. If I don't, I'll bring it in tomorrow.''

Dunn thanked him and headed for the Camaro. He wondered if this was folly, if perhaps Annie held no key, after all, to the murder or to anything else. But just now, Brian's locker was rippling around in his mind. He jerked open the car door, swung himself into the driver's seat, and switched on the car phone. Reaching the postmaster on the third ring, he asked: ''Mrs. Nevins, this is Gabe Dunn, Salem Police. We spoke this morning. I should have asked earlier, but do

your carriers have lockers at the post office? Would Bishop
have had one?''

She answered: "Yes, as a matter of fact he did. It's still
padlocked, I think, but we would have the master key.''

"Find it. Give me a half hour . . . I'll need to get a
warrant signed.'' Dunn hung up and turned on the ignition.
Luckily, Myles was prompt. He climbed in, orange hibis-
cuses flashing beneath his leather jacket. Dunn put the car
into reverse. He said over his shoulder: "Couple stops before
we eat. Courthouse, post office.''

Thirty-five minutes later, in the presence of the union
steward and the postmaster, a representative from the inspec-
tion service unlocked Bishop's locker in the swing room on
the second floor. They laid the contents out on a table. There
was, besides a spare uniform and rain gear, very little else.
A box of Kleenex, a mug, a small bottle of sweetener. Mrs.
Nevins had brought up the victim's satchel from his bench,
empty now except for a pad of forms and a can of *Halt* dog
repellent.

Dunn went through all the pockets in the clothes. Bishop
appeared to be meticulous when it came to emptying pockets
at the end of the day, with the exception of one in the rain
coat. Folded neatly in the breast pocket was one of the pink
forms from his pad, the kind that say a registered letter is
being held for you at the office. This particular form he must
have changed his mind about. Perhaps the recipient finally
answered the bell and he delivered it after all. The name and
address were filled in, but nothing was checked off and there
was no date. Mrs. Nevins confirmed the street was on Bishop's route. Dunn held onto the form, though he wasn't sure
of its importance. Still, he wondered, as compulsive as
Bishop was, why hadn't he tossed it out?

The name on the form was Thomas Weber, followed by
two letters, *J* and *W*, unless the latter was meant to be an *r*,
for junior? The address was in the Gallows Hill section of

Salem. There must have been a reason the form was saved. It was worth calling on Mr. Weber.

The late-afternoon business had slowed substantially. Dover took a short break and slipped into the kitchen to read a copy of the *Salem Evening News*, still smelling of ink. It had been another mild day. She pushed open the screen door and settled out on the back stoop, the cement still warm from the sun. The lengthening days filled that part of her spirit with joy that had dampened in late fall, when the last of the reds had turned to brown.

Dover scanned the Personals first out of age-old habit, then tossed aside the classifieds. Weeding out the Sports section and the advertising inserts, she leaned back, satisfied finally with her higher titer of news. She indulged herself, scanning every page of the remaining sections in this daily ritual, greedily savoring the moments before darkness.

As her eyes swept past the Obituaries, the entry heading the second column leapt out at her:

"BISHOP—of Salem, March 5, Raymond S. Bishop age 62, of 92 Monument Rd. Salem, husband of Coleen M. (O'Shea) Bishop. Funeral Fri. at 9 A.M. From the Murphy Funeral Home, 26 Cabot St. Salem, followed by a Mass of Christian Burial in Sacred Heart Church at 10 A.M. Relatives and friends invited. Visiting hours Thursday 2–4 and 7–9 P.M. Burial in Greenlawn Cemetery, Salem."

There was no answer the first time they went to the Webers' house. The two men elected to finish their quest for Big Macs and agreed to call it dinner. The second visit was more fruitful. The door was answered by Mrs. Weber, a quiet, anxious-looking woman in her fifties, short and plump. Soft, ashen hair accentuated the roundness of her face. Her small gray eyes appeared more used to smiling but now held back. The trace of caution in her stance seemed to clash with an otherwise matronly affect.

"Hi, my name is Gabriel Dunn, I'm a detective sergeant with the police department. This is my partner, Jake Myles. We're here as part of an investigation into the death of a man found at the Willows yesterday. We would like to speak to you. Mind if we come in?"

They were shown in, obviously interrupting preparations for dinner. A man's silhouette appeared in the kitchen doorway. Holding a jar in one hand, he turned rigid for a moment, then relaxed and asked: "What is this about, Officers?"

Dunn turned to him: "Are you Thomas Weber?"

The man nodded.

"Mr. Weber, did either you or your wife know a man named Ray Bishop?" Dunn asked.

Myles dug out a picture and handed it to the couple.

The two looked at each other, then at the photograph. Turning back to the policemen, Weber said: "No. Should we?"

"He was your postman." It seemed a simplistic way of describing a man's life. He could have said, he was a vet. He was a husband, a homeowner, a dog owner. A fence builder. He was a bully. He was a good provider. He was reliable, he was a tyrant. He was an asshole. But the only link he knew of to the Webers' lives was the pink post-office package-delivery form. "He hadn't had this route for very long. We have reason to believe he may have delivered a package or registered letter here a few weeks ago. Do you remember any such delivery? You probably would have signed for it."

From a low part on the left side of his head, Weber's thin, wispy red hair was combed upward in defiance of gravity and nature to cover the extended forehead of its owner.

Sunken dark eyes were fixed on Dunn's. "No, nothing. I never really notice our mailman. We're both at work when he comes."

"How about on Saturdays?"

Weber shook his head. "No, what's happened?"

"Mr. Bishop was found dead yesterday. Do the initials *J W* mean anything to you?" Dunn inquired.

For a moment he froze, but it quickly passed. "I'm afraid not. Sorry we can't be of any help."

Mrs. Weber's hands had begun to tremble. Self-consciously she blurted out: "That's terrible, that man dying . . ."

Explaining that it was a formality, Myles took down their phone numbers and places of employment. He asked if they could remember any of their movements the weekend of March 3. The Webers generally stayed home on Saturdays and had probably watched TV. On Sunday they might have gone to the mall, but couldn't be sure about that particular Sunday. "Please call us if any of it comes back to you," Myles said and handed them a card.

"What the fuck are they hiding?" he asked Dunn as they headed back north.

"I don't know. Let's do a little checking around." Dunn dropped Myles off at the station, then pulled out again. He had an appointment in Peabody.

Chapter 10

Dies supremus musicae

The day the music ended

Annie's teacher lived in a mobile home in Peabody, a somewhat more affluent city to the west of Salem, affluent with the exception of its mobile-home parks lining both sides of Route 1. After interviewing Mel Isaksen at the school, Dunn was unprepared for the teacher's domicile. He wasn't sure exactly what image he had conjured up on the strength of what he had seen of the woman at work, but it certainly wasn't a mobile home.

"I apologize for the lateness of the hour," he offered when she pulled open the door. With the light behind her she looked like Miss Norway in a goat cheese advertisement.

She smiled the smile that had seemed so wasted in a classroom. "It's all right." She showed him in.

"You said today that Annie had been upset recently. Acting up?"

"She's been rather more aggressive toward the other kids than is normal for her. Also, she's had a problem settling in each day—getting down to work."

"When did this begin?" he asked.

"I checked her folder after you left this afternoon. We keep data sheets on each child's work and often add comments or observations if we think it will help explain changes in performance. Annie started deteriorating early this month. She wouldn't cooperate at all on March fifth, so we have very sparse data that day. Sometimes our kids just have bad days, especially on Mondays."

"A lot of us do," Dunn said. His eyes relaxed, dropping the tough, impassive interview look so well ingrained in a cop.

"Well, anyway, I wrote a short note to her father about it, but when it continued the next day, I called him after work."

"What did he say?" He leaned forward.

"At first when I asked him if anything was going on at home, any problems, he said no, none that he could think of. But then I mentioned that she had been signing 'stop' and 'music' for the last two days. He remembered that her tape-player had broken over the weekend and thought that was probably the reason she was upset."

"Did you think he was right?"

"Well, I accepted it at the time. It sort of made sense that she could have been saying 'music stopped.' Also it is true that many of our kids get upset when music's taken away from them. It's as strong a motivator as food for them. Sometimes greater. But thinking about it later, it struck me that Annie had been avoiding music for two days. Not only was she refusing to work to *earn* it, she was pulling off the headphones whenever we simply made it available to her."

Digesting this for a moment, he asked: "What else does she like besides Peter Gabriel?"

"She's not particular when it comes to style. She likes all kinds of things."

"And she still avoids it?" he asked. The teacher nodded. "And this never happened before?"

She replied: "Not in the two and a half years I've known her."

Dunn sat back. "Is Annie capable of telling us if she saw anything?"

"She could, if she has the right words or signs. Asking her directly won't work, though. She won't understand a question about the past, not that far back."

"You mean she wouldn't remember?"

"She'd remember all right. But how would she know we wanted to talk about two weeks ago, not about this morning? We tried asking her why she was angry. She's not at a stage where she can communicate that, however."

Not many of us are, thought Dunn.

> *Hide me under the shadow*
> *of thy wings.*
> —Psalm 17:8

"You mean new names, everything?" Lila asked, fighting back tears. It was around nine Tuesday night. Her husband had switched off the TV.

He nodded.

"What are we going to do about Chris?" Their twenty-nine-year old son was working as a carpenter in North Carolina.

"We'll contact him somehow. When we're settled. We'll find a way to keep in touch with him, Lila. I promise."

"Tom, listen. We may be jumping the gun," she pleaded. "If the police had more than just a name they'd have said so."

"What makes you think that? They're not going to tip their hand to us."

"Their questions would have been different. They were trying to find a connection."

"They had more than just the name 'Tom Weber.' They had 'Jack Wiley.' "

"Just the initials. They can never trace them to you. Tom, we can make preparations. But let's please not go unless we have to. We've been safe here for so long. We get just the one threat, and now he's dead. All he left behind was a name. And the police may conclude it was a package delivery."

Weber looked at his wife. "This is a bad idea, Lila. A bad idea." He paused, then said: "But we'll give it a day or two. See what happens. But let's start planning for it while we can. Lighten the load. We may have to leave in a hurry."

Lila got up and went into the bedroom. Unsure of where to begin. Unsure of how to pack ten years of life into the trunk of a car.

When Jack Wiley was Neil Walton he met and married Lila Marie Kane in Alhambra, California. It was late October 1957. Wiley was easily spooked in the early days of their marriage. They moved frequently and went under a variety of names for a while, none well established. Changing identities was easier for them then. They were young.

Wiley had confided in Lila when they were engaged. Nevertheless she was not deterred. Three years later, under the names Brad and Laura Woods they had a son. Christopher Woods was born in early 1961 in a suburb just outside of Philadelphia. His parents managed to overcome their fears for the next nineteen years, moving twice but keeping their identity. Chris's childhood had been a stable and relatively happy time for them all. Wiley's past threatened to catch up with him in 1980. Chris was living on his own, then. The pair fled without warning and without time, but thankful that their son would not have to flee with them, thankful that he would never experience what they had to experience.

They had managed to keep in close contact with Chris, who had since moved to North Carolina, escaping the harassment and questions. Wary of phone taps they had worked out alternative systems for keeping in touch over the years.

She remembered that last time, how she had felt like a refugee. Food left in the kitchen. Clothes in the dryer. The worst were the photo albums and the boxes in the basement. Boxes containing Chris's childhood: baby clothes, drawings from school, outgrown skates, pieces of a train set.

Nothing could ever be as bad as that time. Tom had picked her up from work one day and said they couldn't go home. With a sweater over her shoulders, her purse, her remains of lunch in a brown paper bag, and a Tupperware catalog she had borrowed from a friend at the office, Lila followed her husband to Massachusetts.

Chapter 11

Ich will euch trösten,
wie einen seine Mutter tröstet.

As one whom his mother comforts
I will comfort you.
　　　　　　　　　—Isaiah 66:13

"Good morning, Mr. President! This is Joe and Andy from the Joe and Andy Show!" Walter Pellegro slammed off the radio which had erupted by his pillow. This was the third time he had hit the snooze button. He and Annie had had another rough night, another nightmared night. A couple of times a week she still woke up screaming. He desperately wanted to call in sick, for both of them. Even the prospect of getting her ready for school this morning was more than he could bear.

Pellegro stumbled to the bathroom, then to Annie's room. Praying the driver would be late this morning, he helped his daughter get dressed. Both of them had to recycle socks from the bathroom floor. Pellegro was out of butter so handed her plain toast while he packed whatever he could find in the refrigerator in a bag and hoped it would pass for lunch. Mel would give her some peanut butter, he reassured himself. The Travel Management station wagon pulled into his driveway.

Pellegro stuffed the child into a jacket, helped her into the backseat, and, with one muscular arm, thrust the small brown paper sack at the driver. "This one's Annie's. Remember!" he growled.

The driver took the bag and tossed it onto a heap of bags by his side.

"They're supposed to have your kid's name on it. We can't be responsible . . ."

Pellegro turned to his daughter and blew her a kiss. He knew parents should consider themselves lucky if the drivers just remembered to drop their wards off at the right school.

With leaden eyes he watched them back out and accelerate down the street. *Slow down*, he wanted to shout, *for chrissake's slow down*. His mind felt like fur, his teeth like glue. He wanted better for Annie. Better than this. Better than dry toast and Travel Management. But mostly he wanted sleep.

Wednesday morning was spent trying to locate Sally Matsamoto, the Salem State student who baby-sat Annie Pellegro the night of the third. Unfortunately, the school was in the middle of spring break, and no one seemed to know where Sally had gone. Myles had checked Thomas and Lila Weber in the computer and found nothing. Nothing in either NCIC or LEAPS, the local analog to the national computer bulletin service. Board of Probation showed no listings. Nothing from the Registry of Motor Vehicles beyond basic registration and license entries. He was halfway through the thirty-four Mackeys in the Salem phonebook and had unearthed none who knew Ray Bishop. Shortly after eleven Dunn came up from downstairs. He took a seat behind his desk, which faced Myles and a shirt out of "Miami Vice." He looked at the younger man, hoping for some news.

"A morning of dead ends," Myles said wearily. "Billy said you were down in the garage this morning. Go through Bishop's car? I listed everything in the report."

"Mmmh, still gotta do that. Actually, I had a rendezvous with the wife of that guy Fagan we busted last week."

"We seized his Pontiac?"

"That's the one. Remember all the toys in the backseat? Turns out one of the bears was critical. Particularly missed."

"And her husband wasn't?"

"She didn't say anything about him. But she had tears in her eyes when she talked about her kid's bear. So I told her to come back this morning and we'd try and arrange something. He's going to need a little restitching after what Billy did to it, but at least he was satisfied enough to release it." Billy Trinidad was the evidence officer. He was strict.

Dunn leaned forward and opened a folder, changing the subject. "The neighbor to the west of the Bishops is a Mrs. Gerard Lufkis. Eighty-eight Monument Road. She's good friends with Coleen Bishop. Thought I might have a talk with her this morning. By the way, the medical examiner's releasing the body this afternoon. Bishop's being waked tomorrow. Funeral's Friday morning."

As they stood up, Myles asked: "So, what'd we get in return?"

"Return for what?"

"The bear."

Dunn pointed to his wall. "A thank-you drawing."

For Lila Weber, life was now a giant game of musical chairs. Every time she left the house, she risked the music stopping before she could return. Lila had begun to pack a box of things to ship to their son. Things she could do without, but not live without. She tried to feel lucky to be given this time. In fact, it was torture.

Lila thought about where they would go this time. She remembered the poverty and isolation, extreme isolation, they would have to endure for a while. You keep to yourself a lot when you have a past to hide. Until you build some history in a new town, there's not much to talk about at parties. You never talk about the place you just left. Like you were from outer space.

Tom always handled the business end of moving. In Salem, his first purchase ten years ago had been a used type-writer, his second, a blank Certificate of Merit form from a local stationery store. Thomas Weber's history and first piece of ID had begun with an Employee of the Month award from Atlantic Contracting, dated May 8, 1980. In a visit to the local library, his name had been culled from the obituary page of a 1934 *Salem Evening News*, which had reported the death in infancy of one Thomas Gordon Weber of North Salem on March 14.

On his way back to the motel, Weber had stopped at the Salem City Hall to purchase a copy of the birth certificate for two bucks. Then he had returned to the library and obtained his library card. Within two days he had procured a plastic ID from a local health club, a driver's license, and a new social security number. A mail order credit card was on its way, and the typewriter was getting heavy use putting out references. By the end of the week they had left the motel and had gotten a room somewhere that was unlikely to check the pasts of boarders. Weber had learned to pick his first jobs with companies equally uncurious. He had been gainfully employed before the cash ran out.

Before leaving for her noon shift at the store, Lila called and canceled a dentist appointment, cleaning out her calendar the way she had cleaned out closets the night before. She shut the clasp on her small overnight bag and loaded it into the trunk of her car with the box for UPS. Returning for one last look, she decided on impulse to shut off the phone answering machine. She didn't want any unanswered messages on her conscience if no one came home tonight.

Lila had started life in Salem as a waitress in a lunchroom with an owner sympathetic to the difficulties of a housewife just entering the work force. In reality, not only had Lila always worked, she knew that without social security she'd be in the work force the rest of her life.

Neighbor Marietta Lufkis had apparently been Coleen Bishop's haven for many a storm. Never needing explanations, she threw together pots of tea or served up glasses of wine, whichever she felt the occasion called for. Coleen often said nothing, just sat and watched her move about the kitchen, brushing aside her dark pageboy bangs, and every few minutes flashing a toothy smile at her two-year-old son stationed under the table. Marietta was the perfect wife and mother, comfortably keeping everything together while her husband was on some archaeological dig. Flipping through Spiegel catalogs while the soup came to a boil, she made every minute of her life count. Here there was peace, the kind working women have to treat as a luxury, as a special moment, but women like Marietta live the peace and miss the treat.

Surprisingly, Mrs. Lufkis did not hold Coleen Bishop's disclosures in confidence. She was more than willing to talk to Dunn, putting into words what he had seen in Coleen Bishop's face. In recent months the marriage had gone sour, partly because the anger which Coleen expressed at 88 Monument Road, couldn't be expressed at 92.

"I told her time and again she had to learn to fight," Mrs. Lufkis explained. "Everyone finds their own way of coping, I suppose. Fighting just wasn't hers." Incongruously, she wrinkled her face into a grin.

"What *was* her way of coping?" Dunn asked, fixing his eyes on her teeth.

Marietta Lufkis paused a long time before giving herself permission to continue. She examined him a moment through heavy-framed glasses. "She's having an affair."

"With whom?"

"His name is Eric. Eric Something-or-other, Whittaker, Whittier. He's an artist sort. Lives on a farm in Topsfield, I believe she said. Though he may well not be for long. He's having some difficulties with the payments." Again, the grin. She was the kind of speaker who underscored the implication of her words with exaggerated facial expression, like a second-grade teacher. But the sort who makes one expression serve all purposes, the expression of an animal in fear.

"When did the relationship begin?"

"I'm not entirely sure. A year, perhaps? She didn't tell me for a very long while."

"Was Mrs. Bishop planning on leaving her husband for this man?"

"I don't think she had made up her mind yet. She finds comfort in security. This man Eric doesn't sound any too secure."

Despite the grin, Marietta Lufkis obviously felt secure. Her husband was two thousand miles away, gone for months. And yet he was here.

"Mrs. Lufkis, could you tell me if you remember seeing either Mr. or Mrs. Bishop at any time during the weekend of March third?"

The woman's head swiveled as her son emerged from under the table and darted behind the couch. "Donnie," she said as he passed by. If she had a verb in mind she soon forgot it. "Not to my recollection. Coleen was at her sister's. She told me that when she got back. She came over here Monday afternoon to see if I knew where Ray was. I hadn't seen him all weekend."

The child reappeared from behind the couch holding a sock in one hand and a spatula in the other. Squatting down in the middle of the rug, he lay the sock down carefully and began to poke it with the spatula.

"Did you happen to notice whether there were any cars in the driveway that Saturday or Sunday? Any come or go?"

"I don't have a good view of the driveway, and I'm sorry, but I wouldn't really remember unless there was something out of the ordinary."

"What's he doing, your son?" Dunn finally had to ask.

"Frying eggs."

He stared at the intense expression on the child's face and found himself believing it. He smiled and stood up to go.

Picking up her son, she accompanied him to the front door. "I hope you don't suspect Coleen of anything like . . . murder. She's incapable of anything like that. I wouldn't want you to misconstrue what I've told you, Sergeant."

"You've been very helpful, Mrs. Lufkis." Dunn wondered if Coleen Bishop knew how really loyal a friend her neighbor was. "Please call me if anything else comes to mind." He handed her a card and she followed him out to the car. As he climbed in, she studied the ground as if deciding whether to speak.

The toddler began to squirm. "Naptime," she announced in a singsong voice. With a swift movement she rotated the child in her arms, and carried him back to the house upside down. He in turn rewarded her with peals of outrageous laughter. Dunn watched them with envy for a moment, then switched on the ignition.

At the station he picked up Myles and they headed for Topsfield.

Quaint, he thought. A hippie. The man wore shoulder-length, pewter-gray hair and one of those shirts from Africa which showed up at cocktail parties in 1970 and had a name we all knew back then. Gaunt face, mid-forties. Sandals, no socks, and something with leather around his neck.

Eric Whittier led them inside and pointed to the living room. The house appeared to be a couple of hundred years old, a mixture of authentic old-world craftsmanship and twentieth-century deterioration. Exposed beams and beautiful detailing framed crumbling plaster interspersed with the tell-tale holes of blown-in insulation.

Half expecting his host to sit on the floor, Dunn took a seat by a large bay window, leaving Whittier and Myles the couch. To his relief, they both sat on it.

"How long have you known Coleen Bishop?" Dunn asked.

"I couldn't tell you exactly. I don't keep a calendar."

No, of course not, thought Dunn. He was beginning to wonder if Whittier would be a hostile witness, when the man stretched out his thin legs and added: "I guess it's been about ten months."

"How did you meet?" Dunn doubted it was an insurance claim. The unlikelihood of these two people ever occupying the same space or even the same time seemed overwhelming.

"There's a festival and craft show every year on the Salem Common. I go each time to sell mirrors." To Dunn's questioning look, he continued: "I take old window frames and replace the glass with mirrored glass. They sell pretty well. Last May Coleen came by my booth and bought one."

"When did you next meet her?"

"She took one of my cards. Said she was interested in seeing more of my work. So a week or so later she called me. Came up, I made her some tea, and we talked."

Dashiki, Dunn remembered. He asked: "About what?"

"Not really your business. Let's stick to facts. Pertinent ones." The serene look in the man's face never changed. One of those guys left over from the sixties who refused to display anger. Myles, whose own shirt paled by comparison, shifted in his seat and waited for Dunn's response. There was no way to force this line of questioning.

"To your knowledge, did her husband know she was seeing you?" Dunn met the serenity with impassivity.

"Not to my knowledge."

"Do you have any recollection about the weekend of

March third and fourth?'' Dunn asked, and braced himself
for the calendar line again. He wished he had called this one
down to the station, onto his turf. Interviews went smoother
when it was your doll and dishes.

"That would be the weekend Ray disappeared?"

"That's right."

"Coleen was in Gloucester at the time. I was here working
all weekend."

"Did you talk to her at all?"

"She called me Saturday to tell me where she was and
that she was coming back Monday morning."

"Did she mention arguing with her husband?"

"With Coleen, the problem is not the arguing, it's the not
arguing," Whittier explained. "She was going quietly crazy
living with him. She went to Gloucester to decide what to
do about it."

"And what did she decide?" Dunn asked.

The man turned unblinking and strikingly blue eyes toward
the detective. "We'll never know, will we."

"Mr. Whittier, do you think Coleen Bishop could have
killed her husband?"

"What motive could she have? Wouldn't divorce have
been less strenuous?"

Dunn replied, "Money. Life insurance, perhaps, and his
estate. The house must be paid off by now, and if he didn't
agree to a no-fault, she probably would get very little in a
settlement."

"In answer to your question, I don't think Coleen would
be capable of murder for that reason, or for any other."

"How about you?" Dunn asked.

Whittier smiled, unperturbed. "I didn't kill Ray Bishop,
Sergeant."

"Nice place," Dunn remarked as they got up. "Do you
own it?"

"Me and the Bank of New England," the man replied.

When the men had left, Eric went back out into the barn. Flipping on the radio, he resumed his seat on a tall wooden stool at the workbench. Unheated except for a bronze-colored quartz heater in the corner, the room had grown chilly. Eric pulled his jacket on. From the small round speakers of his radio ushered forth a familiar Led Zeppelin riff. *Soul of a woman was cre* . . . *ATED below*. Eric smiled to himself and bent down over the mirrored glass. Taking up his glass cutter he began to score.

Chapter 12

Recordare Jesu pie,
Quod sum causa tuae viae;
Ne me perdas illa die.

> *Recall, merciful Jesus,*
> *that I was the cause of your journey;*
> *do not harm me on that day.*
> —Requiem "Dies irae"

Myles was the one with the contact at the bank. One of the security supervisors at the Bank of New England was a retired cop from Peabody. Myles had helped him out on some case a few years back. The two had been in touch a few times since, and Myles had shown up at his retirement party. Within a half hour he had the loan history on Eric Whittier. Not admissible in court, but useful.

Coleen was studying the first of the sympathy cards to show up when Dunn and Myles rang the doorbell. They announced that a few more questions had come up, but that they would try not to take too much of her time.

"Mrs. Bishop," Dunn began when they were seated. "Could you tell us about your relationship with Eric Whittier?"

She seemed unsurprised at the question. Whittier must have called to warn her, he thought.

"I've been seeing him occasionally since last summer." She fixed her gaze on the card still in her hand. As if reading from it she added: "He was a friend to me. I had no intention of leaving Ray, if that's what you're thinking."

Dunn's voice was steady: "We've just talked to the Bank of New England. They tell us that on March fifth Whittier came in to make his mortgage payment, which was in arrears. In fact, the bank had threatened foreclosure. Whittier brought it in cash. Do you know where he got the money?"

This time she looked surprised. "No!"

"Did you give it to him?"

"No, I did not. He would never have asked me for it, nor would he have accepted it. He must have sold some of his work."

"Over one weekend? He was unable to negotiate a partial payment the week before."

"It could happen. Maybe he got a tax refund. Is this important?"

Dunn began to think it was. "One more thing, Mrs. Bishop. Have you ever heard the name Thomas Weber before? Or Lila Weber?"

She shook her head.

As the door closed behind them, Dunn noticed the postman coming up the driveway. Recognizing the man as one they had questioned the previous morning, he smiled and waved. "Running late?" It was nearly three o'clock.

"Not at all. This is my usual time. It's the end of my route."

For a second, Dunn was surprised. Why had he imagined the mail would have come in the morning? As they stepped down from the porch, a question started to nag him. If Monument Road got their mail in the afternoon, what was on the floor when Mrs. Bishop returned home at noon, Monday March 5? They continued down the brick path, Dunn in silent thought. The sounds of passing cars reminded the neighborhood that the winter hiatus in traffic was drawing to a close and that soon warm weather would bring crowds and vehicles in constant pilgrimage to the Willows.

Just then, Dunn heard Marietta Lufkis's muffled voice calling out her son's name from next door. He detected alarm in the faint sound and stood still, listening. Suddenly he spotted Donnie Lufkis's tiny body barreling down their driveway toward the street. Like a runaway bus, his stubby little legs propelled him with terrifying momentum, his red curls lifting in the breeze.

Dunn sprang into motion. With a few quick bounds he reached the front fence and catapulted himself over. Donnie had crossed the sidewalk without slowing, eyes fixed on the far side of the street and an objective known only to himself. The policeman sprinted straight for the child, and, looking up, glimpsed to his horror the sun's reflections in the chrome grillwork of a red Dodge Caravan rounding the bend and doing fifty.

Jake Myles leaped out into the street behind him and began shouting and waving at the driver to slow down. Dunn's eyes were glued to the boy. As the distance between them decreased, he reached out his right arm. In one heart-stopping second he scooped up the child and twisted around toward the curb. The van never slowed, and its right mirror grazed him on the shoulder as it sped by. He fell to the street, cradling the toddler. As the van moved off, he could hear through its open windows the Doppler effect shifting the music down in pitch. Somewhere behind him a woman screamed.

Donnie began to howl. Marietta Lufkis had emerged from the backyard in a frantic run, but now stood frozen on the lawn, hands to her mouth. All color had drained from her face.

Dunn sat up, his chest pounding violently. "Get him, Jake. I'm all right," he whispered. But Jake had left.

* * *

Dunn refused the offer of a trip to the emergency room
and returned to the station. The shoulder would probably be
worse the next morning, but for the moment he was alive,
or a close approximation thereof. Myles had nailed the van
down by the entrance to the park. He had radioed for Hurd,
and when the cruiser arrived, Myles had three youths spread-
eagled against the side of the van and, in defiance of policy
and good judgment, his Smith & Wesson drawn. Hurd had
come with backup, and Myles relinquished the kids and a
few illegal items from the van.

Sitting now across from Dunn and finishing a Mars bar,
he took longer to describe the chase than the chase had taken.
"On top of the 'operating to endanger,' we got a real good
'driving under' case."

Dunn scowled. "Patrol supervisor complained about the
gun. You gotta watch it, Jake."

"Reinhardt's a fucking asshole. Clueless. You know that
as well as I do. He wouldn't see an armed robbery if it were
on the hood of his cruiser. Know what?"

A dull ache was beginning to spread throughout his shoulder. Dunn tried to rotate it, preferring pain to ache. "What?"
he managed to say.

"Two of the guys are good friends of Kyle Raider, the
kid down the street."

"So, is there supposed to be some connection?" Dunn
was losing interest in the van incident. And he had no incli-
nation to learn how Myles had extracted this information.

"Well, his uncle did have a beef with Bishop."

"And? Why take out Donnie Lufkis?"

Myles leaned back and stroked his chin. "Maybe the
Lufkis kid saw something he shouldn't have."

Dunn stared at him a moment and said very slowly:
"Good. Good work, Jake."

Myles popped the end of the Mars bar into his mouth and

stood up. As he reached the open door, Dunn said: "Wait, Jake. Listen, how tall would you guess the boyfriend, Eric Whittier was?"

"Dunno. About my height, I guess. Why?"

"Close enough to Bishop . . . he was five seven. What are you, five eight?" Dunn asked.

"Eight and a half." Myles resumed his seat. He wadded up his candy wrapper and shot it into Dunn's wastebasket.

Dunn pulled out the bottom drawer of his steel-gray desk and propped a foot on it. Bottles of white•out rolled to the back. "If Whittier were wearing Bishop's jacket, maybe with a bit of extra padding, and had a muffler wrapped around his lower face, and was wearing a hat . . ."

"What the hell are you talking about?"

"Saturday. Outside Pellegro's window. Walter Pellegro got only a brief glimpse as the guy got into the car and drove away. Through a window cluttered with plants, through a chain-link fence. And he would, of course, expect it to be Bishop. The mind often sees what the eye does not."

"Why don't you think it was Bishop?" Myles asked. "We only have one clue to his whereabouts for the whole weekend. Now you're trying to blow it off."

"I'm just saying, we can't take anything for granted. Pellegro says he saw Bishop Saturday afternoon. Either he saw Bishop, and Bishop was alive then, or he saw someone who looked like Bishop."

"Or he was lying," Myles added.

"Or he was lying."

The two were silent for a minute. Then Myles asked: "So what are you thinking?"

"Maybe, just maybe, Coleen and Eric conspired to kill her husband."

"Motive?"

"Oh, usual stuff. Love, hate, money. Not a lot of money. But people have been killed for less. I'm wondering if maybe

Coleen helped Eric out with the mortgage payment. I looked over some of the Bishops' recent bank statements. Coleen loaned them to me with his stuff. She made a couple cash withdrawals that weekend, the weekend of the third.''

"Go on," said Myles. "Wouldn't that leave a trail? It *did* leave a trail."

Dunn smiled. "Of course. And from the handwriting on the back of the other statements, Ray Bishop usually balanced the checkbook. I wonder what he would have said about the withdrawals. If he had lived to see the records."

The younger man frowned. "Doesn't the lady strike you as having been terrified of her better half? Why would she risk . . ."

Dunn tried to give Myles a look he could appreciate. "Maybe, just maybe she knew he'd never see the statement."

"Let's ask her about the withdrawals!" Myles slapped the desk.

Dunn answered softly. "No. I already returned them. I want to be careful, Jake, in case we have to subpoena them later."

"OK, OK. So why would Whittier dress up as Bishop Saturday afternoon?"

"Throw the time of death off. Maybe he had an alibi after that. And taking the car to the station would make it seem like Bishop had left town, presumably of his own volition. When you got the missing-person call, what did you think had happened?" Dunn asked.

"That he booked. We all did. Especially after we heard about their argument Thursday night. That's usually the answer, guy wants out."

"Right. You put up a pretty good show for her, though. Understand you went through their garbage," Dunn said with admiration.

Myles smiled. "And you can bet it's all in the report. I considered heat-sealing it and sending it down to ten-ten."

Dunn got up and began to pace. "But let's keep in mind the alternatives. Bishop was alive or Pellegro lied. OK, Jake, why would Pellegro lie? Could he have killed Bishop? What's his motive?"

His partner shrugged. "Maybe he was really pissed off about the fence. I would have been."

Dunn looked at him. "You wouldn't have killed the guy."

Myles leaned toward him and said menacingly: "Maybe . . . maybe I would have killed his little *dog*."

Dunn stared back at him. "You would, wouldn't you." He pulled the phone toward him and dialed Coleen Bishop's number. After a dozen rings he replaced the receiver. "All right, Jake. Will you find out about the dog? Someone's gotta know something. There's one other person who probably wanted that dog dead."

"Raider," Myles answered, shoving a finger in Dunn's face. He stood up, flashed his best Raymond Chandler grin and sauntered toward the door. Interrupting his second exit, he turned and looked questioningly at Dunn. "Wait a minute. Whittier didn't mention any alibi today."

"I suspect Whittier is cagier than we think. I wouldn't be at all surprised if one comes out of the woodwork next time we chat with him. I'd bet a lunch on it."

Chapter 13

Hostias et preces tibi,
laudis offerimus.
Suscipe pro animabus illis,
quarum hodie memoriam facimus ...

We offer to you in praise, o Lord,
sacrifices and entreaties.
Take them for the souls
we hold in memory today.
—Requiem "Offertorium"

The gray Lincoln Continental had been impounded late on the evening of March 5, shortly after its discovery at the train station. Still covered with a layer of snow, it had been photographed and towed. Mrs. Bishop had come down to identify the vehicle. She also had provided a set of keys.

The car was still down in the garage. Wednesday evening after Jake left, Dunn went downstairs to look through it himself. He could see the usual jumble of maps, a couple of scraps of paper, a glove, an ice scraper. Cars seem to suck debris from their occupants, he thought. They entrap anything of any size that can be wrested from us. Thermoses lodge beneath its seats. Hairpins, quarters, pens pile up in every crack. Small bits of foil, even if you don't chew gum. Coffee stirrers, empty sugar packs. Crumpled tissues, gas receipts, parking lot tickets, car wash coupons. Unidentifiable but critical plastic and metal parts, often carefully saved in the glove compartment. Small flashlights, usually several, that don't work, and a spare fuse, or a blown one.

Bishop's car had surprisingly few of these items. It struck Dunn that the debris in one's automobile seemed inversely proportional to one's age, and that one of the requirements for retiring seemed to be a spotless car. By this measure, he could estimate this driver to be sixty-two or -three.

Carefully he slid into the driver's seat, avoiding the steering wheel with its fresh dusting of powder. Out of habit Dunn reached for the brake with his foot. It seemed a bit far for his comfort, and Bishop was three inches shorter than he was. Possibly the seat had been moved back when Myles or the print man went through the car. Dunn began his search.

The maps were mostly local—Boston downtown, Massachusetts, New Hampshire, one badly worn of Danvers and Peabody. A popular road atlas of the Boston area, with the most critical pages missing. Such is the fate of all road atlases when one lives or works on one of its pages. An automobile club map of New York City, also old. The maps all had a flattened dead look about them that suggested they hadn't been opened in a while. Like clothes you haven't worn in five years and can't now because hanging in the back of your closet they've had the life squeezed out of them.

Dunn turned his attention to the assorted scraps of papers that were clues to this man's life, or possibly to his death. Much in that category seemed indeed to be part of the common denominator of all drivers. Anything that had dates he piled chronologically on the seat beside him. An ATM slip from early January didn't tell him much—a hundred-dollar withdrawal. The balance printed on the slip seemed uninteresting. Part of a grocery list, too faded to be relevant, contained nothing more potent than Pepsi—six-pack—and no date. He pulled out a parking lot ticket from the visor and looked at it closely. The ticket was for the indoor lot at the East India Mall. Dunn felt a brief moment of excitement. The ticket was time-stamped 7:42 P.M. Friday March 2. Although Bishop hadn't been reported missing until the following Monday, the ticket gave a tangible glimpse into Bishop's last days. Of course, he couldn't be sure Bishop was the one who parked the car, and he needed answers to the obvious questions: when did the car leave the lot and why wasn't the ticket turned in?

Dunn slipped the ticket into his pocket. Upstairs he retrieved the photos of Bishop and the car, and the cassette that Brian Hurd had left on his desk.

It is said that Wednesday night is singles night at the Purity Supreme. For the rest of the world, it is spaghetti night. Six-fifteen was a bit early for any action, however, and anyway, Tom Weber wasn't single. The man at the checkout counter towered like a linebacker above Weber's small frame. Weber had been selective in his purchases, only buying a few meals at a time now. Small-size laundry detergent. One can of coffee. A box of Clairol hair coloring. The checker brushed the Clairol box over the sensor and glanced up at Weber's balding pate. Weber squinted through thick glasses as the price flashed above the register. And the word "tint." It always began with "tint," their new lives, now up to $5.49 a box.

"So how about those Bruins, hey?" said the linebacker, as he passed the coffee can along with a wrist shot.

Weber peered up at him. "I don't watch the Bruins. Sorry."

"Oh, what's your game? Did you catch the Celtics?"

Weber gave a smile of impatience and looked back at the Tide, whose turn had not yet come. "Nope. Didn't catch them."

The man looked down at him in disbelief.

"Patriots? Red Sox! Baseball's your game!" he announced.

Weber shook his head apologetically. The Tide shot past. "I don't really follow any of them."

The man leaned back and hooted with laughter. "Man, the women must be all over you!"

Dunn left the Camaro in front of the station and took his own car home for the night. Since it was on the way, he decided to take a look at the mall. At quarter to seven in the evening he knew the place would be dead. Except for the moviegoers, milling around just before showtime. And the restaurant.

Officially renamed "Museum Place" in an effort to resuscitate business, the building nevertheless mirrored Salem's economy and had steadily declined in occupancy. Half the storefront windows were covered with paper. The halls and food court were empty and cold. Even the bookstore, one of the mainstays of the place for years, no longer found it profitable to remain open evenings.

The remaining commodities were geared more and more toward the tourist trade. Not particularly proud of its past, Salem had nevertheless been forced to capitalize on the witchcraft hysteria in order to survive. Creative marketing approaches managed to give a kind of Disneyland packaging to the present-day practice, much to the chagrin of the city's current witches. Halloween was the one day in the fiscal year when the city went into the black, so to speak.

Dunn, whose own badge depicted an old woman on a broomstick, still thought of the building as the East India Mall. He turned into the entrance to the lot and punched the large button. A ticket offered itself. He glanced at the time stamp. A sign on the booth indicated that his first hour was free. After that the damage was fifty cents an hour, with a daily maximum of four dollars.

The patrons of the cinema tended to use the outdoor lot on the north side of the building. The ramp ahead of him stretched upward into darkness. Not a car was in sight. Dunn had no trouble finding a parking place. He nosed his Chevy up to the door of the stairwell. The satisfaction of having the best lit, most convenient place, free for one hour, almost made the trip to the mall worthwhile. A good parking place was like a good cigar.

Dunn pulled open the heavy door and followed the stairs down to the main floor of the mall. From the dank and uninviting cement stairwell he emerged into the hallway in front of Lotus Gifts, which was open. The proprietor within looked up from his book at the sound of the door. Dunn looked down the hall in each direction. After the parking lot the bright lights made him blink. Bright lights, splashy displays, hopeful signs. But no customers. Like a stage before curtain.

The detective toured the first floor and took note of who and what was open. Next to the movie theater was a video arcade, with signs of life. Not the kind of life that would do the mall much good, though. Out of several food concessions, only one bothered to stick it out until the last show started.

Dunn first checked with the theater manager to find out show times for Friday, March 2. All four films started between seven and seven-thirty. The next showings were two hours later. With slim hope he showed the photograph of Bishop he was carrying to each of the staff. Maybe one of them knew him. Maybe Bishop had picked a fight. They each shook their heads.

Dunn repeated the exercise at Roy's Gyros and back at Lotus Gifts, each time with no success. That only left Weylu's.

"Good evening! One for dinner?" the waiter asked, picking up a red leatherette menu.

The detective thanked him and declined. "I'd like to speak to the manager."

The waiter gestured to the cashier.

Mr. Chen had been managing this branch of the highly successful chain of Boston-area Chinese restaurants since it opened in the mall a decade ago. Dunn had been an occasional patron for as many years, and recognized the man.

"How may I help you this evening?" he asked.

Dunn showed him the picture and introduced himself. "Have you ever seen this man before?"

Mr. Chen studied it for a moment, then said: "Yes, sir."

"You know him?"

"He comes in now and then." He took another long look at the photograph, then seemingly reaching into some vast card file in his mind, added: "His name is . . . name is Bishop."

"That's correct. Any possibility you'd remember if he came in on March second, a Friday?" Dunn asked doubtfully. "Perhaps he charged dinner."

The man smiled. "Too many people come in here." He gestured toward the bar where patrons sat waiting for their names to be called. "But I can look through the slips for you." The young woman beside him was filling out a bill. He turned to her and said something in Chinese. She nodded. He came out from behind the counter as she took his place at the register.

The business office for the restaurant was across the hall in a former shop. Dunn followed the restaurant manager as he unlocked the door and went inside. Whatever filing method he used must have been effective. The receipts for March 2 were located within a few minutes. Mr. Chen separated the credit card slips from the bundle and lay them on the desk. There must have been two or three dozen.

They split the stack and each searched for Bishop's name. Both came up empty. Dunn handed his stack back and turned to the rest of the bundle. "If Bishop paid cash, you'd have no record, right?"

"We'd have the bill, but no name. That's right. Unless he ordered something to go."

"You keep the names of the take-out orders?"

"Whatever name they give us when they call it in, we write it on the order."

Dunn nodded toward the bundle. "Could we check?"

Bishop had indeed called in an order to go, and luckily had not been creative when he gave his name. Spicy chicken with orange sauce, pork fried rice, and an egg roll. Mr. Chen translated the order out loud. Circled in the upper right corner of the order form was the time it was called in. Seven-thirty P.M.

On the way out of the garage Dunn handed his ticket to the man in the booth. The first hour had indeed been free.

"What time do you get off duty?" he asked the attendant.

The man looked startled. Lest it sound like asking for a date, he rephrased the question:

"What time does the booth close, like on Friday nights?"

The man was still suspicious. "Why? You can still get out. The gate's left open."

Dunn showed his badge, then handed over the photographs. "Ever see this guy? Or the car?"

"I'm not good with faces. I see too many of them."

"He came into the lot a couple weeks ago. Friday night, March second, around quarter to eight."

"I don't see them when they come in."

Dunn retrieved the pictures. "Do you always see them when they come out?"

"What d'ya mean?"

"This guy's ticket was never turned in. I need to know

what time he left the lot. When did you say you open the gate?''

The man smiled. ''Like I was saying, I leave after the last show lets out. Probably around eleven-thirty.''

''And if this guy left before then, how could he have gotten out without giving you his ticket?''

''Might have lost it. He pays me four dollars. I let him out.''

Dunn shook his head. Bishop didn't strike him as a man who lost parking lot tickets. And Myles's report said the ticket was stuck in the visor, in plain view. ''I don't think so.''

The man was quiet for a minute. Then he lowered his voice. ''Well, sometimes, once in a while, I need a break. Short, you understand.''

''I understand. How do cars get out while you're gone?''

''I leave the gate up. After the evening shows start, things are pretty quiet till they end. Most people use the outdoor lot for the restaurant.''

But the indoor parking garage was more convenient if you were coming from the Willows. Dunn caught sight of two headlights reflecting in his rearview mirror as a car started slowly down the ramp toward him. He was blocking the exit. Until now they had been utterly alone. Dunn turned back to the attendant, who began to look agitated. He asked: ''Would you by any chance remember taking a break on March second?''

The man's eyes were fixed on the headlights. ''Yes, I believe I did. Yes.''

''What time, and for how long were you gone?''

''I . . . probably seven-thirty.''

Dunn waited. The car was on his rear bumper, revving its engine. In a second it would honk.

The man continued: ''I would have been back by eight-thirty. No later.'' He had been holding Dunn's ticket the whole time. Now he glanced down quickly at it, then stabbed at some register keys. "All set, mister."

The digital display outside the booth flashed $0.00. The gate began to lift and Dunn shifted into drive. "Thanks," he said to the attendant.

The car behind him honked.

Chapter 14

I stand alone without beliefs
The only truth I know is you
 —Paul Simon "Kathy's Song"

It was Thursday morning. Dunn had wasted a half hour coaxing and swearing at his Chevy Impala. The morning was damp. He should have anticipated the wires would be. He rued once again, as he did almost weekly now, not making the break with this monstrosity. Not old enough to be camp, it was still a rarity to find a large American station wagon such as this one on the road these days. A true family car, with a front end built like a tank for protection, room in the rear for twenty bags of groceries, including the cart, and seat capacity for six legally, twelve illegally. The previous owner, Dunn's brother-in-law, had once removed the rear seat and housed his Honda 450 inside. A family car with no family.

Dunn had acquired the car, at the time only four years old and still recognizably gold in color, a month after his daughter was born. It had been an act of charity on the one hand, since his sister Rachel needed some cash. But at the same time, Dunn had considered it an action of a Responsible Man, providing a vehicle more appropriate for his expanding family than the rusty MG he selfishly had clung to. They immediately bought an infant car seat, rated safest by a leading consumer magazine. Dunn installed it in the right rear seat. For over a year after she left him, taking their ten-month old child with her, Dunn couldn't bring himself to remove the seat. Even though his daughter, now five, outgrew it years ago, it probably would be there still, except for his being pressed into service one day to ferry seven members of the Salem Police Department softball team to a game.

Finally Dunn gave up. Directing his words to the Chevy, he said, "I don't have time for this now," slammed down the hood, and biked the mile to the police station.

As he slipped into the office, Myles gave him a smug day-is-half-over look. Looking at his watch, he said: "We've got this case nearly solved. How's the shoulder?"

"Just great," Dunn growled. The internal line chirped in response. The desk announced that a female calling herself Mrs. Bishop was here to see Dunn. "Send her up," he said.

A few minutes later, there was a tap on the open door, and Coleen Bishop was shown in. Dunn pointed to the seat by his desk, into which she settled down.

"What can we do for you?" he asked.

The woman gazed incredulously around the office before answering. Fundamentally, the place looked like a turn-of-the-century schoolroom. A Hearne Bros. map of the state was mounted high on one wall, and a cardboard Dracula face, left over from some Halloween, was taped to the door through which she had just entered. Seven steel-gray desks and an assortment of neo-Salvation Army cabinets and office appointments stretched down its length. Dark wooden supply shelves which might have held scissors and crayons instead were crammed with police radios, blank warrant forms, and an anatomically correct doll. The walls above each detective's desk displayed their individual interpretations of the car repair bays at Gordo's Jiffy Lube. Coleen's eyes skirted around a vintage Marilyn Monroe calendar, discreet but unmistakable in its message. Like credentials in a doctor's office. These guys were Men.

Unsettled, she checked her rain-abused hair in the tabletop mirror on Myles's desk. Etched onto the glass were the outlines of Clint Eastwood's mug overlooking the end of a pistol barrel, and the inscription, Feel Lucky, Punk? Not particularly reassured, she straightened her skirt and at last let her eyes meet Dunn's. She wasn't feeling very lucky.

"You asked me earlier if I had heard of Thomas Weber. I said I hadn't, but I think maybe I have. Something peculiar happened a week before Ray disappeared."

Dunn nodded for her to continue.

"It was Saturday. He was delivering on his new route. When he got home he was all excited. Wouldn't tell me why at first. But he dug out an old photo album and started going through pictures from his war years. After a while he must have found what he was looking for, because he suddenly yelled out, 'Jack!' "

"Did the name mean anything to you?" Dunn asked.

"No. I asked him what it was about, and finally he told me. Ray said he had known this guy in Korea. Apparently he got in some serious trouble and disappeared. Ray never saw him after that, until that Saturday. Said he goes by 'Weber' now and that he was running from something. Ray felt sure of it."

"What did your husband do about it? Did he call the authorities?"

"No, at least I don't think so. This is hard for me to say, but I think he may have considered blackmailing Weber."

"What makes you think that?" Dunn asked, without changing his expression.

"Well, for the rest of the weekend he seemed to be enjoying the discovery, enjoying the power the knowledge gave

him. He didn't talk much to me about it, but he was preoccu-
pied with it. I don't think he was spending all that time
thinking about calling the authorities.''

"Do you have any evidence that he contacted Weber after
that, or that Weber contacted him?''

"Not directly, no. It just struck me that the possibility
was very obvious, and that it would occur to Weber, too,
whether or not Ray did plan to blackmail him. I think uncov-
ering a secret like that could endanger your life. And Weber
apparently was no stranger to trouble.''

Mrs. Bishop opened her purse. "I brought the picture. I
thought it might help.'' She handed it across the desk to
Dunn.

Dunn squinted hard at the black-and-white print. It had
scalloped edges and was still glossy. The contrast was poor
and the images unsharp. Nevertheless, on the edge of a group
of about nine uniformed men stood, unmistakably, a younger
Thomas Weber.

"Mrs. Bishop, did he mention a last name?''

"No, not that I remember,'' she answered, knitting her
brow.

After she had left, Myles whistled and said: "So what are
we waiting for? Let's scoop him!''

"Slow down, Jake. What happened to 'means' and
'opportunity?' ''

"His only alibi Saturday night is his wife, and they
weren't even positive about what they did that particular Saturday. He was a soldier, so we know he's capable of
killing.''

"What about the weapon?'' Dunn mused.

Myles responded with sarcasm. "Blunt instrument. Not
too many of those.''

"One blow. It takes a lot of strength to kill with one
blow.''

"Weber doesn't strike me as a weakling. He's on the small side, but I think he's strong enough," Myles offered.

"Maybe." Dunn stared longingly at the cigarette in Myles's hand. "Her story's going to have to be verified. And even so, we're still going to have a problem with the alibi. We're saddled with an indeterminate time of death. Without an iron-clad alibi for the entire weekend, anyone can be considered to have had an opportunity. But let's start with what alibis we do have. Let's find that baby-sitter. I want to know what upset Ann Pellegro. I want to know who besides Coleen Bishop benefits from her husband's death. I want to know how her dog died. And I want to know how prone Mr. Raider is to violence. And his nephew, the kid with the gash on his head. And who the hell Mackey is. Come on, we've got work to do."

Myles stood up. "Shouldn't we talk to Weber?"

"Not yet. If what she says is true, he's likely to bolt when he learns he's been made."

"So we arrest him."

Dunn's impatience was growing. He rubbed his shoulder. From the doorway he asked: "Come on, Jake . . . on what grounds? Take that photo with you, Jake. You can do the Army part. Aren't they still looking for a few good men? I'll take Salem State."

"That's the Marines," Jake grumbled. That's what you get with a cop who can't read.

Chapter 15

Quaerens me sedisti lassus.

Seeking me, thou sat down weary.
—Requiem "Dies irae"

The registrar's office at Salem State College provided Dunn with the address of Sally Matsamoto's dorm. Dunn mounted the steps of what was once a nineteenth-century mansion on Lafayette Street and rang the bell. It took a good five minutes before the only resident to be at home figured out no one else was answering the bell. Footsteps pounded down from the attic bedroom. The girl, canonical student in sweatshirt and jeans, flung open the door. She showed Dunn into a high-ceilinged, sadly misappropriated parlor, now containing a pool table, TV, vending machine, and two plaid couches. The dark-hued woodwork was gorgeous and looked original. Each of the tall front windows was bordered with small panes of leaded glass in rose and amber. Adorning one of the center panes were two decals: one saying Salem State, the other of the cartoon character, Bart Simpson.

Dunn took a seat, removing a Diet Pepsi can from between the cushions. "I'm trying to locate Sally Matsamoto. I understand she lives here. When we called her number we were told she had left on spring break."

"That's right. She left last Friday night."

"Do you know where she went?"

"She and a friend were going to drive down to Florida. Fort Lauderdale."

"Does she have family down there?" Dunn asked.

"Fort Lauderdale?" She looked at him like he had two heads.

He tried again: "Did she leave an address or number where she'd be, or of places where she might stop on the way?"

The concept seemed to take her by surprise. She shook her head.

"Has she called here at all? And who did she go with?"

"Her roommate Theresa. Their room's on the floor below mine. I have the single in the attic. Yeah, they called here, musta been two nights ago. They were in some motel somewhere, having a wicked good time."

"Any idea where? Did they mention the name of the motel?"

She thought a minute. "They had made it to Florida, I think they said. But were too tired to drive any more that night. Somewhere just over the state line. I think they were on Route 1. They shoulda made Lauderdale the next day."

"When is she due back?"

"Classes start next week. Knowing Sally she'll be back at eight that Monday morning. Or a few minutes after."

Dunn asked for a picture of the girl, and left instructions to ask Sally to contact the police if they should call in again.

"Why are you sticking around during break?" he asked at the door.

"I'm in the chorus. We've got a spring concert coming up. We're rehearsing every day." She looked glum.

"Is this Ralph Mackey?" Myles had nine names to go. But then there were six Mackies. He wondered if Bishop could spell.

"This is Detective Myles from the Salem Police Department. Did you by any chance have an appointment to see a man named Ray Bishop on Thursday March eighth?" Nope.

He dialed Richard Mackey. "Richard? This is Ray Bishop. Did I miss our meeting the week before last?" He had completed the lower left corner of his desk blotter and began extending short, fine pencil strokes up the left side to where the number for Domino's Pizza was scrawled. The design looked like something between a woodcut and a porcupine. "Bishop. Ray . . . Sorry? Oh, I guess I dialed the wrong number."

The next number did not answer. Myles filled in the "o" in Domino's.

The drive up to Gloucester took just under a half hour. Coleen's sister and brother-in-law lived only a few blocks from the highway in a two-story house with pale-blue aluminum siding. Junipers clung to each corner, connected along each side by neatly trimmed privet hedges. The men mounted the steps and rang the bell.

Angela Robinson was heavier and taller than her sister. With an unfaltering gaze from beneath her high forehead, and a mouth set with opinion, her face contained the strength that Coleen's lacked. Her hair was pulled back with barrettes; not a wisp remained untamed. Even her polyester pantsuit said "this woman will not wrinkle."

Dunn and Myles stepped into the dark front hall. At the far end, Dunn could not help noticing a framed mirror hanging on the wall. The frame appeared to be from an old window. He smiled, and at his expression Mrs. Robinson commented: "Special, isn't it? Coleen gave it to me. She thinks it's art."

"What do you think?" Myles asked her. She laughed scornfully.

The men were led into the living room, overly filled with rococo furniture, and ordered to sit.

"The man was an animal," she started, unasked. Dunn wondered if she ever answered questions or simply issued statements all her waking hours.

Dunn tried anyway, during the fleeting second in which her lips pressed together to underscore the word "animal."

"Do you mean he was physically abusive to her?"

"No. He didn't hit her. He didn't have to. You should've heard him yell. Like a Marine sergeant. And when he wasn't yelling he spoke with a voice that would freeze your blood."

"And she put up with it?"

"My sister's a wimp. She was absolutely the wrong person to live with a guy like Ray. If I'd been his wife, he would have been out the door in a week. Mostly I'd have yelled back. But I wouldn't have put up with the boozing. And no amount of a wife's yelling could have changed that part of him."

Probably true, Dunn thought. "Why did she stay with him?"

Her sister shrugged. "She didn't have the backbone to fight back, and she didn't have the guts to walk. I suggested it, of course."

"Mrs. Robinson, we need to ask you about your sister's visit the weekend her husband disappeared. When did she arrive, when did she leave, and was she with you the whole time?"

"Well, I didn't do a bed check during the night. She slept in our guest room. But other than that, yes, we were together. We spent Friday and Saturday shopping, gabbing, errands, things like that. Sunday we stayed in the house all day. Except for Mass. My husband and I went to Mass in the morning."

"Did Mrs. Bishop go with you?"

"No. She doesn't usually go to Mass."

"How long were you gone?"

The woman thought for a second. "Oh, about two hours, maybe a bit more. Our church is about a fifteen-minute drive from here. We have friends up there and we meet them for breakfast beforehand."

Salem's an hour round trip, Dunn reminded himself.

"And she was here when you returned?" he asked.

"Yes. She was in the kitchen reading the paper."

"And what was she doing when you left earlier?"

"Well, she was asleep. I didn't bother her."

Dunn sat back. "Are you absolutely sure she was in her room?"

"How could I be? I told you I didn't check her bed."

Chastised, Dunn regrouped. "Where was her car when she was here?"

Mrs. Robinson thought for a moment. "She had to park on the street. We only have room to pull in one car here."

Myles looked up from his notebook and asked: "Did you notice her car when you left for Mass?"

She sat in silence for a moment. The steady gaze never faltered, but it was as if a cease fire had been called. The lips tightened and relaxed a few times, until finally she made up her mind. "I'm sure it had to have been there. But I don't remember looking at it. I was helping my husband back the car out."

Dunn glanced at Myles, who bent back down over his notebook. He turned again to the woman. "Mrs. Robinson, could your sister have left her room during the night without your knowing?"

The woman looked surprised. Then she shook her head. "Impossible. The guest room's on the second floor. The stairs creak and my husband's a light sleeper. Also, the front door has to be slammed to shut properly. We both would have heard that."

Dunn said: "Couldn't she have used the back door? Gone

out through the kitchen? If your husband heard her on the stairs, would he have told you?''

"When he wakes up, I wake up. Without fail. He doesn't say anything, just grunts and sighs. He falls right back to sleep. I'm left staring at the ceiling for an hour. I would have heard even the back door. She didn't leave during the night, Sergeant, I assure you.''

Dunn asked to see the room. Mrs. Robinson led him upstairs and pushed open the door of a small bedroom. Each wall was papered in a different pattern. Moving to the window he estimated the height to the sill to be easily reachable without a stool. He undid the latch and carefully swung open one side. Sticking his head out, he noted there were no convenient drainpipes or other obvious methods of escape. Finally he took a close look at the sill itself, and decided the layer of dirt and dust, bearing the marks of spattered raindrops, had not been disturbed in a long while.

Mrs. Robinson began to show impatience. "If you gentlemen have nothing further, I have to get ready for the wake.'' Dunn glanced at his watch. Taking a last look around the room, he thanked the woman, signaled to his partner, and the two men took their leave.

Myles drove in silence for several minutes. Finally, he asked: "Could Coleen Bishop drive back to Salem, whack her husband on the head, drag the body in daylight to the men's room at the Willows, and drive back to Gloucester by the time Mass ended?''

"Unlikely, not impossible. Pull into that ADAP," Dunn said suddenly.

"What is it this time? You should open a fucking account with them," Myles replied with irritation.

"I just need a set of wires.''

When Dunn returned to the car, Myles turned down the radio and shifted into drive. Merging into traffic he asked, as he always did: "The car, Gabe. When?''

And as he always did, Dunn responded: "Soon."

Dunn took out the box of wires from the plastic bag and forced himself to read all six surfaces. The Chevy warded off the hubris, he thought to himself, kept his nerve endings raw, his senses keen. Kept him tough. Kept him compassionate. Whenever his character headed off with too much determination in one direction or another, this car maintained the contradictions, maintained the balance.

Chapter 16

Gere curam mei finis.

Take my demise into your care.
—Requiem "Dies irae"

People were filing in whom Coleen didn't even know. Letter carriers, probably. Since it was a closed casket, Ray's cousin Alma had suggested a picture should be placed on the top. The woman had somehow turned up a framed photograph of Ray taken about twenty years ago. Coleen felt increasingly uncomfortable. She hadn't known Ray when it was taken, and she found it somehow distasteful, having it perched there on the gleaming wood. It reminded her that his life was, for the most part, not their life. It also reminded her of why the casket was closed.

Ray's brother was leaning forward in the chair beside her. She rarely saw Robert when Ray was alive, perhaps once a year or less ago. The last time had been a wake, too. Robert's wife's. She had begun to feel a sense, a slight sense, that he was family then, once it was over. As if in-laws are brought closer by funerals. Closer by degrees.

Under Robert's chair was an unopened bottle of Jack Daniel's and a carton of cigarettes. They were meant to go in with Ray, to be laid beside him on the pink satin. But of

119

course, now they couldn't. Robert hadn't realized the coffin would be closed.

"I forgot all about it when we last talked. I was at an arts and crafts show all day Sunday. Up in Ipswich. I can show you the receipt for my table if you like."

The policemen had detoured through Topsfield on the way back from Gloucester. "That won't be necessary. We believe you, Mr. Whittier. And what about Saturday night?"

The man appeared to be struggling for a moment. Finally: "How important is this, Officers?"

"How important is staying out of jail?" Myles answered.

Oh Jake, Dunn thought to himself. But he let it go. Jake Myles wasn't the only master of theatrics present.

Whittier paused, then said: "I was with a lady."

Of course you were, asshole. Myles gave Dunn a knowing look. "Let me guess . . . you spent the night in her embrace and she went to the craft show with you . . . Sorry, *art* show in the morning."

Whittier looked glum. "Close enough."

"She always did have a fondness for art."

Dunn stepped in. "Thank you, Detective Myles. Mr. Whittier, we'll need the lady's name, if you don't mind. And Mr. Whittier, we ask that you please not leave town during the next few days without notifying us."

When the door had shut behind them, they turned and walked back down his driveway, the gravel crunching beneath their feet.

"So where am I taking you to lunch?" Myles asked Dunn.

The store where Lila Weber worked was called Ruby Doux. It was part of a string of gift and specialty shops in the Vinnin Square Plaza, on the line between Salem and Swampscott to the south. Ruby Doux specialized in plastic-

ware apparently. Dunn threaded his way between columns of
red-and-white stacking shelves to the cashier halfway back.

The man behind the counter was in his late forties. His
face and hands looked scrubbed clean and pink. Dunn asked
for Lila Weber and was told politely that she was on a break
and should be returning in a few minutes. A few feet from
the counter a younger man was busy pricing plastic tape
measures in bright shades of mauve and green.

Dunn decided to wait. He wandered toward the rear of the
store and amused himself by guessing at the purpose for
some of the more mysterious items, each available in popular
colors. Aside from him, the store was devoid of customers.
He picked up a pair of angular wire forms, advertised to be
"shelf dividers," and speculated as to the possible improve-
ment in his life they might bring. Perhaps he could get rid
of some of his bricks.

All at once, the cashier began to sing. In a baritone that
was clearly not amateur, snatches of *Rigoletto* filled the store.
At first, Dunn wasn't sure if it was the radio or the man,
but after each line or two, the singer paused and conversed
with the youth. The detective was slightly unsettled; since
the conversation was clearly private, the opera must have
been as well. Thus, rather than applaud, he busied himself
with some tumblers. The man jumped into *I Pagliacci*, interspersed with explanation for the pricer's behalf.

Finally, the claustrophobia Dunn was beginning to feel
among so much white polyurethane overpowered him and he
headed for the counter, shelf dividers still in hand. The cashier smiled.

"Anything else today?" he asked, reaching for Dunn's
selection.

Surprised, Dunn had forgotten that he still had them. He
relinquished the package, and as the man began to ring them
up, the detective said: "I enjoyed the *Rigoletto*."

The man beamed. To the boy he said: "See? *Every*one knows *Rigoletto*. What did I tell you?"

To Dunn he said quietly: "In this life I'm learning patience. One does what one has to while one waits to do what one wants."

Dunn smiled and pulled out his wallet. The baritone was struggling with the cash register and finally asked the boy for help.

"Ya gotta put in the department code first," the kid said, and coming around behind the counter, he poked at the keys. All of a sudden a small printer beside the register sprang into life.

"Shit," said the kid. "It's coming out sideways."

Dunn looked at his watch. The printer was slow, maybe twenty words per minute. "I really don't care which way it's printed," he said politely.

"No, you see, when it's sideways it don't total. We'll get you another one . . . only be a minute."

I only bought one fucking item, Dunn thought. *I don't need a total*. "I don't really need a receipt," he said. "These aren't under warranty, are they?"

"Oh, yes!" said the baritone. "One year!"

The three of them stared at the printer as it grated away in a high-pitched whine. Finally, the singer pulled the receipt out carefully and handed it to Dunn. The boy went back to his tape measures.

"You'll like these shelf dividers . . . they're marvelous!" the man said sonorously.

Dunn managed a smile and made his escape.

Outside in the fresh air he selected a bench on which to continue his wait, but before he reached it he spied Lila Weber emerging from the Brigham's Ice Cream next door.

This was not the fun part, said Jake Myles to himself. He had emerged from the District Courthouse with a few printouts and some more pages filled in his notebook. Walking the few short blocks back to the station, he stopped off at the Home Plate, pushed open the door, and found himself a large table near the window. He ignored the menu and opened his notebook.

The waitress was new, and gorgeous. Myles smiled at her. He ordered his usual chili and corn bread, with a Coke. This was the fun part. Reluctantly, he turned back to his day's results. No other lawsuits against or involving Bishop. No court records on Thomas or Lila Weber. None on Dale Raider, Walter Pellegro, Coleen Bishop, Eric Whittier. Earlier queries on the Board of Probation computer had turned up an assault charge on Kyle Raider, the nephew at Raider's address. Myles had also uncovered a speeding complaint. No city department had handled the disposal of Bishop's dog. Nor had the local vets. If that was worth pursuing he'd have to go back to Mrs. Lufkis. Army intelligence had never heard of a Thomas Weber matching that guy's description. Or a Jack Weber. Jack "W" they couldn't help with.

When she finally brought his order she had forgotten the corn bread. He forgave her and asked her for a date. She laughed lightly and declined, saying a girl had to be careful nowadays.

"You'd be safe with me, sweetheart. I'm an officer of the law. 'Serve and Protect' . . . that's my job." He resisted the impulse to flash his badge.

Before he made detective, Myles had been a real street animal, a tough, aggressive cop. Now he stroked his jaw, as if to check that it was still square, that his face was still hard. He was still shot down. And no corn bread.

Recognizing the policeman, Lila froze. Dunn walked up to her. She looked for a moment like she'd been hit.

"Mrs. Weber?" he said. "Can we talk a moment?"

She nodded with a heavy expression. They found a bench

and sat down. Resting an arm along the back of the bench, Dunn asked, without looking at her: "How long has your husband been blackmailed?"

She said nothing. Both stared straight ahead. Her grip tightened on a small paper bag clutched in both hands.

"Personally, I'm not interested in why. I need to know if it was Ray Bishop."

After a moment she spoke: "I can't help you, Sergeant."

Dunn stood up. Looking down at her, he said softly and without sarcasm: "You have my sympathy, Mrs. Weber. I imagine it must be difficult for you."

He turned and headed for the parking lot. By the time he stepped out into the curbside lane she had caught up with him. She touched his arm. Dunn stopped. Her eyes were filling with tears and he led her back to the curb. Silently, he offered her a handkerchief.

"Can we . . . can he get some kind of immunity? Can I talk to you in confidence?"

"I can't make you any promises, Mrs. Weber. I can't give you immunity from anything. I certainly can't force you to talk to me. I will talk to the DA, if it's any help."

For a moment she broke down. He put an arm around her, then walked her to his car, away from the crowd, away from the windows of Ruby Doux. Settling her inside, he let her cry.

After a few minutes, she forced herself to regain composure. She studied his handkerchief. As if finding the answer there, she said: "Tom was contacted. Once. The weekend you asked us about. He said Bishop wrote him a couple days before. Then called him Saturday night and arranged to pick up the . . . money."

"What time was the call?"

"I'm not sure."

"How long was your husband gone?"

She said, barely audibly: "I wasn't there. I was helping a friend. I got back close to midnight."

"Was your husband there?"

"Yes."

"When did you leave to go to your friend's?"

"Around eight or eight-thirty. Tom was home. I don't remember any calls before I left."

"And he was absolutely sure it was Bishop?" Dunn asked.

"He told me it was. But he said the voice sounded disguised."

Dunn stared at her. "Disguised? Then how . . . what made him think it was Bishop? Did he see him?"

She returned his gaze. "No. But no one else kn— no one else had reason to blackmail him."

"I'll need to talk to your husband."

She winced. He added: "I don't need to tell him I talked to you."

"No, it's not that. I'd tell him we talked. It's . . . he may not talk to you. He may be afraid to."

"Maybe. I have to try. I'm looking for a killer, Mrs. Weber." He reached for his keys. "Would you like me to take you home?"

She shook her head. "No, that's all right. I'm OK. I have to go back to work."

Dunn got out and came around to open the door for her. As she stepped out she added: "Tom is . . . incapable of hurting anyone. He didn't kill your Mr. Bishop."

"Hasn't he hurt you?" Dunn asked.

She looked him squarely in the eye. "Never. I could never wish for more than I have with him."

He watched as she crossed the lot and disappeared into the store. Climbing back into the Camaro, he started the engine and pulled out. Lucky man, he thought.

Chapter 17

Ingemisco, tanquam reus.

I groan as one who is guilty.
—Requiem "Dies irae"

Thomas Weber made much of his living as a self-employed bookkeeper. On Thursdays, according to his wife, Weber spent the day at Baldwin's Carpet Sales in North Salem. Although Mrs. Weber was working late, she had said her husband should be through by five-thirty. Dunn went directly to Baldwin's from Vinnin Square. He pulled into a spot from where he could see the front door, threw a Copland tape into the machine, and waited. It was 5:26.

Halfway through the *Nocturne*, Weber stepped out the front door. Dunn slid out of his car. He strode to the sidewalk as Weber approached. Swinging open the passenger door, he said: "Mr. Weber? I need to have a word with you. We can talk in my car or we can talk in front of Baldwin's."

Weber got into the car.

"I want to know what happened Saturday night, March third. The night your wife was at her friend's."

The man was silent. Dunn continued: "I have two sources who have indicated you were blackmailed. Is it true?"

"I don't have to answer that."

"No, you don't. I don't have to charge you, either. But if you leave me no choice . . ."

"Charge me with what?"

"With the murder of Ray Bishop. You're my prime suspect."

"You have no fucking grounds!" Weber hissed.

"I have witnesses who will testify . . ."

"You can't make Lila testify against me!"

"Not all my witnesses are married to you, Mr. Weber. Also, I've got a photograph. And you've got a motive. And no alibi. Means and opportunity, Tom."

"I didn't kill him."

"No, of course not. Now tell me why I should believe you."

Weber got control of himself. "All right. Bishop sent me a note. The Wednesday or Thursday before. He said I had until Saturday to get two thousand dollars in cash together."

"Bishop? How do you know?"

"The timing. He ran into me by accident the weekend before, when he dropped off our mail. Four days later, I get a letter. It couldn't have been anybody else."

"Do you still have the note?"

"It's at home."

"I'd like to take a look at it. What happened next?"

"He called, like he promised. Saturday night."

"Did you know Bishop's voice well? Or did he identify himself?"

Weber shook his head. "I didn't remember his voice that well, no. But the voice on the phone was strangled and whispered. I wouldn't have recognized it anyway."

"Why do you think he bothered to mask his voice, knowing you knew who he was?" Dunn asked him.

"Maybe scared I was taping him."

"Were you?"

Weber laughed sardonically. "Yes."

Dunn stared at him. Weber continued: "I thought that if I had proof on tape, that I'd have something on him. In case he ever bothered me again. But with his voice disguised, I ended up with nothing."

"Well, not necessarily. Disguising his voice wouldn't affect the voiceprint if we have the tape analyzed. It might not be conclusive enough to convict, but it would be very useful in court."

"Can't convict him of anything now," Weber said ruefully.

"What time was the call?" Dunn asked him.

"Just after nine, if I recall. Nine P.M."

"What did he say?"

"He told me to go to Forest River Park. And to drop a Filene's bag with the money into the first trash can in the parking lot. At ten sharp. Come alone, leave immediately, just like on TV."

"What did you do?"

"Exactly as I was told. Except that I went back around ten-thirty to see if the money was gone. I didn't want to throw it out if something had gone wrong."

"Was it gone?"

"Yes."

"Did you see anyone?"

"No."

"And where's the tape now?" Dunn asked.

"Home. With the note."

"Let's go." Dunn reached over and opened the passenger door. "I'll follow you."

Someone had fixed Coleen a plate from the buffet and brought it into the living room where she sat, stiff-backed, on the edge of her chair. Her sister and brother-in-law had drawn up chairs beside her. Angela was talking about the trees in Greenlawn Cemetery. Ray's brother was at one end of the couch, sunk deep into the corner, working silently on his cold ham.

In an hour they would have to go back to the funeral home for evening visiting hours. Then two more hours, plus some minutes of politeness, minutes when her sister would settle Coleen in for the night, probably offering to stay, but Coleen would decline the offer. Then she would be alone.

Coleen looked around. She was still holding the plate of untouched food in her hands. She felt like she was the lead part and had forgotten her lines. The rest of the cast were cleverly rewriting the script as they went, and writing her out. Then she remembered it was Thursday. The fourth Al-Anon meeting in a row she was going to miss. For a brief moment it flashed through her mind that she should go. At least to explain why she'd missed these past few weeks. And to say that anyway her problem had solved itself.

Weber led him into the living room. In a corner was what appeared to be his "office-in-home"—a couple of two-drawer file cabinets supporting a desktop, a heavy-duty calculator, boxes of forms, stacks of canceled checks, ledgers, pencils, bookkeeping paraphernalia. Weber went over to the desk, pulled out the lower left file drawer, and bent down. He slipped his hand beneath the drawer. Tearing at what sounded like tape, his hand reemerged with a white business-size envelope. He handed it to Dunn.

Dunn lifted the flap, which was not sealed. Inside were a sheet of typing paper folded in thirds and a microcassette tape.

"Has anyone else handled the note?"

"No one."

Dunn carefully removed the cassette, then with his handkerchief lifted the note out and unfolded it. It read:

"Jack: Remember Korea?
$2000 in cash buys my silence.
Have until Saturday.
Will contact you with instructions.
Don't worry. I won't bother you again."

"Could we listen to the tape?" Dunn asked. Weber
popped open the cover of his phone answering machine and
switched tapes. Then he hit the *play* button.

The quality was abysmal. It was a cheap answering machine. The call sounded like it had been made from a public
phone in an intentionally noisy environment. The voice was
indeed distorted, hovering around a raspy whisper with an
attempt to feign some sort of accent, at least sufficiently to
cover any regionalism. Most of the talking was Weber's,
repeating and clarifying the instructions. The voice on the
other end had to specify Forest River Park twice. The rest—
the time, the drop point were clear enough, and as tersely
spoken as possible. Then the caller hung up.

"I'd like to borrow this. If it is Bishop, it helps us establish when he was alive."

"And if I killed him, it establishes a motive," Weber
answered. Nevertheless, he ejected it from the machine and
handed it to Dunn.

Sliding the note and envelope into the file folder he had
brought in, Dunn added: "I'll need you to come down to
the station for elimination prints."

Weber shook his head. "Sorry. Can't do that."

Dunn sighed. It would be a lot easier if he could bring
himself to arrest the guy. The alternative was to get a court
order, but the grand jury wasn't convening again till Wednesday. "Don't leave town, Mr. Weber."

It was well past quitting time when Dunn got back to the
office. He made a copy of the letter Weber had given him.

Then he filled out a form for the lab, bagged and heat-sealed the original of the letter and the tape. He wrote out a note to the technician and taped it to the pouch:

> "Check tape for prints and save for later spectrography. Possible use as elimination set for prints found on letter."

Dunn folded the copy he had made of the letter and left it on Myles's desk with instructions to check out the Bishops' typewriter. He doubted any blackmailer who watched TV would use his own machine when the nearest Sears had an aisle full of them you could borrow in peace. The chances of finding a known recording of Ray Bishop's voice were questionable.

Exhausted, the detective went to his desk and collapsed in the chair. In the middle of his blotter was a note from Myles on yellow lined paper in bold, self-satisfied script:

> *"Steven Mackey—lawyer w/ firm*
> *Culbertson, Cheadle and Noyes/Salem*
> *Appt to write/change will. Mackey*
> *thinks RB had none previous, at least*
> *w/ their office. Does not know what*
> *RB's intentions were.*
> *Intestate—wife inherits??"*

Dunn smiled. *Right, Jake.*

Chapter 18

Domine, libera eas
de poenis inferni
et de profundo lacu!

*Lord, free them
from the pains of hell
and from the deep abyss!*
—Requiem "Offertorium"

Later Thursday night, the OIC phoned Dunn at home. Sally Matsamoto had been located. She had apparently come down with the flu or something and was returning from Florida early, by bus. She should be arriving back in Salem Friday evening.

Are we as disappointing to men as they are to us? Coleen wondered. *Where the hell are all the heroes?*

The last of her visitors had left. Coleen checked each phone to be sure all the extensions were on the hook, picking one up every few minutes to hear the dial tone. She walked about the house with arms and chest of lead. With so much to do, it should have been easy to find some distraction. But no other thought could gain a foothold. Her mind would not let go of its pain. The sound of every passing car measured her abandonment.

Eric had said he would call. Even the promise of a call had seemed a letdown to her. Of course, the need for discretion was still important for a while. But the discretion should have been difficult for him, as it was for her. Would a little show of impatience have been beneath his dignity? And now, even the call, even the call had not come. It was quarter to ten in the evening.

Eric didn't drink, didn't yell, didn't watch TV or schedule his evenings around basketball games. His priorities seemed to her to be good ones: his art, his farm, but his priorities didn't include her.

She lay down upon the bed and began to sob. Was there no man on earth for whom she could be the highest, the only real priority?

Whenever he was on a homicide case, Dunn ran out of food. They always seemed to catch him on the very day he had planned to go grocery shopping. Gabe starts a shopping list . . . someone in Salem drops dead. This was his fourth night on the Bishop case and he was getting sick of sesame seed buns. Pulling the phone toward him, he lifted the receiver and with the same hand dialed his sister.

"It's your uncle Gabe," he explained to the voice on the other end. "What are you doing up so late? Put your mom on."

After several long minutes his sister came to the phone. "Rachel, I'm starving. I know it's late. Have you got anything to eat over there? Of course I've been busy. I wouldn't be begging a meal if I had . . ."

He let her give him the lecture about the Ziplocs and the freezer while he went through his mail. The outcome was always the same. Learning about buying in quantity was part of their routine. "I'll . . . Rachel . . . I'll be right over."

Rachel and her family lived in a handyman's special in the historic district of Salem, just off Chestnut Street. The house was still pretty special after four years. It boasted, among other features, two kitchens, the second of which was upstairs and was always about to be converted to some other thing. In the meantime, its cupboards were filled with a mixture of toys, dirty laundry, and canned vegetables, making it indistinguishable from the one downstairs. It always bothered Dunn when, in the middle of dinner, for example, someone would ask where the A-1 sauce was, and his sister would answer, "It must be in the other kitchen." It seemed to him too pat an answer, too perfect an excuse. Rather like having two chances to get your life right: "Have you made your contribution to the United Way?" "No, I'm taking care of that in my other life." Or: "It's OK, Dr. Danbury, I'm flossing in my next life."

In his sister's driveway, Dunn switched off the Camaro, which he had borrowed for the night. Drug dealers' cars were so reliable. When he went in, the kids had been stuffed into beds. Dunn's brother-in-law Warren was in the living room correcting papers. Warren Carlson was a high-school teacher. To Dunn he was braver than any man on the force. The detective followed his sister into the kitchen where she had set out an assortment of aluminum foil shapes.

Opening them, Rachel assembled a plate of meat loaf, potatoes, and gravy and handed it to him. "Wave this for about two minutes." He took the plate and opened the microwave oven door behind him. His sister slid into a seat at the kitchen table. She had brought her book in, in case he didn't feel like talking. "Make yourself a salad. There's stuff in the fridge. Done any flying?"

"I don't need a salad," he said. "And no. No time. No money."

"Make yourself a salad," she repeated. "And you shouldn't let little things get in your way, Gabe."

Dunn tried to remember at what point in their lives their parenting roles had switched. At age sixteen, he had had to take on much of the responsibility for his younger sister and brothers when his mother had succumbed to a pulmonary embolism, particularly since his father worked late hours. Rachel had been both youngest and toughest, wilder than any of her brothers. When she was a senior in high school, the last brother had left home and Rachel found life alone with her father to be strife-ridden and unbearable. After running away twice, she had finally pleaded with Dunn, eleven years her senior, to let her move in with him.

Dunn had almost been dissuaded that year of ever having children of his own. His sister had not been easy, forcing him to invent rules precisely because they had been breached. Times of turbulence gradually gave way to moments of equilibrium, however. Both survived the year and came to depend upon each other. Throughout college Rachel came to him frequently with her problems, but after her marriage and babies, he no longer had any answers for her. Dunn guessed that her mothering must have emerged when his own wife left.

As he neared the end of the meat loaf he said: "Rachel, you have a radio alarm clock, don't you? What do you do on Saturdays and Sundays?"

"What do you mean, what do I do?"

"Does it go off at the same time every morning? Automatically?" His own alarm clock was round with hands and a button that had to be pulled out every night.

"Well, yes . . . I guess on the weekends we're supposed to unset it. We usually forget. Are you thinking about buying one?"

"No. Can I see it?" They went into the bedroom and Dunn spent twenty minutes playing with the clock—how it got set, armed, what happened when it went off, and how you shut it off. When he was satisfied he went back into the kitchen and helped himself to coffee. Rachel remained on the edge of the bed resetting the clock and both alarms to the way they were. As usual, everything ended up off by twelve hours so that the P.M. light was only on in the morning. But somehow they always managed to wake up.

She rejoined Dunn but found her patience thinned. "If you're going to be mysterious, I think I'll go to bed."

Dunn poured her a cup. "I have a time problem."

The chair scraped in response as Rachel sat down.

"I have a dead man. I have an indeterminate time of death. He was indisputably alive Friday afternoon when he left work. He never showed up the following Monday. His car was found at the train station covered with Saturday evening's snow, undisturbed. These I take as facts. Then I have a lot of claims."

"Not all of them true," Rachel said, returning the ball. She yawned. Get on with it, Gabe, she thought. He was scoring the rest of his mashed potatoes with his fork.

After a dramatic pause worthy of Jake Myles, he continued: "If I believe the wife, a man with her husband's voice talked briefly to her Friday night around seven. A parking lot ticket puts the car, or would seem to put the car, in the East India Mall at twenty to eight that night. Someone using the name Bishop picked up a take-out at Weylu's around that time. The wife was unable to reach him by phone over the weekend."

"So what's your problem?"

"The Saturday paper was missing. The Sunday and Monday papers were outside. The wife was out of town the whole time. We have one witness who claims to have seen him Saturday afternoon, and another who thinks he talked to him Saturday night."

"So what's your problem?" she repeated.

"When the wife came home Monday the radio was on. It had turned itself on at six A.M."

"Monday morning?"

"Or Sunday, or Saturday. Whichever it was, he most likely wasn't there to shut it off. Unless he had gone deaf."

"Maybe someone stuck an ice pick in his ear."

Ignoring her, Dunn said. "There are lots of possible explanations, but the most likely scenario is that he wasn't alive Sunday morning when the *Globe* came."

"Or just that he wasn't home."

"True, although he didn't pack for any trips. Now this is interesting. When Jake Myles went over to the Bishops' the day she reported him missing, he, being the frustrated archaeologist, was clever enough to go through the garbage in the kitchen. No one else in the department would have done that."

"What did he find?"

"The top layer consisted of a few beer cans and Chinese-food boxes. We think Friday night he picked up Chinese food at the mall. Below that was a piece of Friday's paper, egg shells and coffee grounds. No signs of any other breakfasts. Below that was stuff that Mrs. Bishop recognized from Thursday night. They never found the Saturday paper."

"You think he died Friday night?"

"The garbage suggests so. But how could he? Why would the neighbor lie? And then there's the blackmail incident. One of my suspects says he was contacted by Bishop Saturday night. The guy was told to make a drop-off, which was definitely picked up. My suspect checked later."

"Sounds like your guy Bishop was alive Saturday night."

Dunn studied the grounds in the bottom of his cup. After a while he said: "The strange thing is, I really can't picture Bishop as a blackmailer. He was a tough guy, temperamental. But staunchly patriotic. Living comfortably. It would have been stupid—he'd have that hanging over him the rest of his life. The victim knew who he was. Would have had a hold over him. I just don't see it."

"Who else could it have been? Who else knew whatever it was he knew?"

"The wife. But she was in Gloucester that night. Two people attest to that."

"So what d'ya got?" she asked.

"I don't know. I don't know what I got."

Dunn changed the subject. "Dad's birthday is Sunday. Why don't you give him a call?"

She looked away.

"Rachel, give him a call." The roles had reversed. He added: "Thanks for dinner." Scraping back his chair, he stood up, leaned over and kissed the top of her head.

Dunn carried his dish to the sink. After attacking it with a few shots of the sprayer, he reached for a dish towel but came up empty-handed. From her seat Rachel tossed a limp red-and-white-striped wad toward him, which his years on the softball team enabled him to snare. "This is sticky," he complained, and dropped it into the plastic laundry basket next to the fridge. "Haven't you got a clean one?"

"Try the other kitchen," Rachel answered.

Chapter 19

Inter oves locum praesta,
Et ab haedis me sequestra.

Gift me with a place among the sheep,
and separate me from the goats.
                    —Requiem "Dies irae"

Early Friday morning Myles talked Dunn into breakfast at
Red's. Red's Sandwich Shop occupied a seventeenth-century
building next door to the station on Central Street. Just as
they finished ordering, the front door swung open and Brian
Hurd entered the lunchroom. They signaled to him. Hurd
approached their booth and settled in beside Myles.

"Did you find the tape I left?" Hurd asked Dunn hoarsely.

"Peter Gabriel? Yeah, thanks. Nice album. Didn't tell me
anything, though."

"What was it supposed to tell you?" asked the patrolman.

Their waitress reappeared with coffee and added Hurd's
breakfast request to the order. Myles yawned.

Dunn responded with a sigh. "I don't know. Some key to
my star witness."

Myles grumbled: "You don't know that Annie was a witness to anything."

"Well, she is a mystery," Dunn said. "Maybe not this
mystery, but a mystery. And there's another one as well."

" 'Behold, I show you a mystery . . .' " Myles intoned.

"What's that?" Hurd asked.

"Corinthians, I think," said Myles.

"I was talking to Gabe."

Dunn answered: "Coleen Bishop. She tipped us off to the blackmail. Why?"

Hurd shrugged. "I was being polite."

"No, Brian, why'd she tip us off, not 'why did you ask,' " Dunn explained. Hurd could be a bit thick.

Myles reached for the sugar. "It seemed a reasonable piece of information to bring to the police in my opinion."

"Very reasonable. So why did she wait four days. Hell, why'd she wait two and a half weeks?" Dunn asked.

Hurd reached across Myles to hunt among the bottles and jars at the head of the table. "What blackmail? Do you see any Sweet'N Low?"

Myles was putting together a response when the waitress appeared. "Who's the sausage?" she asked, with plates balanced up one arm and down the other.

Myles smiled at her. "I'm the sausage."

She turned to Dunn. "No jeans today? Got court?"

All heads turned to stare at Dunn's navy-blue cords. "No. I'm going to a funeral," he said somewhat defensively.

She set down Myles's plate and moved to the next booth with the remainder. Dunn and Hurd leaned over and watched Myles poke open his eggs.

Myles frowned. "So you don't believe she just forgot."

Hurd remembered his coffee and leaned around to the girls in the booth behind him. "Excuse me, could I borrow a couple of your Sweet'N Lows?"

Myles looked at him. "*Sweets* . . .'N Low. Brian, it's *Sweets*'N Low."

"Huh?" Hurd turned to him. The girls started fishing through their jars.

"Leave him alone, Jake," Dunn said. "What was the

first question you guys asked her when she filed the missing person?''

"Any known enemies. Anyone with reason to harm him," said Myles.

Dunn nodded. "She remembered the missing newspaper. She forgot about the blackmail."

Astonished at the intricacies of mass noun pluralization, Hurd was still staring at Myles. "Are you sure?"

Myles looked at him and smiled. " 'We shall not all sleep, but we shall all be changed.' "

Hurd's look changed to one of suspicion. "What the hell are you talking about, Jake?"

"I told you. Corinthians. 'O death, where is thy sting?' "

"How's your wife, Brian?" Dunn asked.

Finally his waffle arrived, followed by Hurd's eggs. The Sweets'N Low flew over from the other booth like tiny pink missiles. The sun poked through on Hurd's face and the three ate a while in silence. Except for the chattering in the booth behind them.

Myles swallowed the rest of his coffee and dug three dollars out of his pocket. "I'm late. I'm supposed to meet Whittier's lady friend. His other lady friend. Wanna come along?"

"No, thanks," Hurd croaked.

"I was talking to Gabe, Brian."

Dunn replied: "Like I said, I've got a funeral to get to. I'll meet you back at the office around lunch."

" 'O grave, where is thy victory?' " Myles said. Hurd stood up to let him out.

Dunn looked up at him. "I thought you only read crime fiction."

"You'd be surprised."

"Nice talking to you, Jake," Hurd said.

"Check ya later, bud."

When Hurd sat back down, he said to Dunn: "She's fine."

"Who's that, Brian?"

"My wife."

Dunn smiled at him. "Good!"

Still, the guy did have a great tape collection.

Requiem aeternam dona eis, Domine:
et lux perpetua luceat eis.

> *Grant them eternal rest, O Lord,*
> *and may perpetual light shine upon them.*
> —Requiem "introit"

It was not Dunn's first visit to Greenlawn. The cemetery, located in North Salem, was known for its trees. Native sugar maple, red oak, birch, pitch pine, hemlock, and a hundred other varieties gave the grounds the appearance more of a park than a burial ground, a place to which one might choose to come, unbeckoned by any other purpose than to enjoy its beauty. But Dunn had come before to bury two of his family: his older brother and, years later, his mother.

Friday morning had started out cloudless and mild, though the forecast was for colder weather by afternoon. Dunn attended the funeral alone, and tried to stay out of the way. As the words were spoken under an inappropriately sunny sky, he scanned the small crowd and took inventory. Mrs. Lufkis, Mr. and Mrs. Robinson, several postal employees he recognized, including Mrs. Nevins. Pellegro was absent, no love lost there, he supposed. Eric Whittier was tactfully absent. Dunn wondered if he was much comfort to her. A brother had come from out of town. Most of the rest were just faces. Somber and composed, briefly considering their own mortality. Composed except for one young woman he hadn't seen before, who stood off at the far edge and had started to weep. It struck him from the intensity of her tears that she might be family, but why, then, wasn't she up with the rest of the relatives? The woman turned then, and strode quickly down the drive.

Dunn caught up with her at the front gate, having peeled himself from the group with the minimum of attention.

"Are you all right?" he asked.

She turned, surprised. Her face was wet, but otherwise quite beautiful. Dunn thought she must be in her twenties. She was dressed in a dark-blue jersey dress with a charcoal jacket for warmth. Bareheaded, her dark hair shone in the sun, and rested lightly on her shoulders.

She clearly wasn't. Dunn suggested she sit down for a while, and they took advantage of a concrete bench alongside the caretaker's cottage. Not knowing if it would make it easier or harder for her, he explained that he was a policeman.

"Did you know him?" he asked her then.

She leaned her head back against the stone wall behind her and closed her eyes. At last she spoke.

"I think he was my father."

Portia Sunkist lived on Route 1 in Topsfield, across the highway from the fairgrounds. Her house looked barely habitable. The yard was an amalgam of meadow and woods, the driveway impassible. Myles parked the car in the parking lot of the feed store next door and made a path to her front porch.

By the looks of the steps, he tread carefully. The porch itself, however, still enjoyed heavy use. Boards were stacked on boxes on either side of the front door and were lined with clay pots in various stages of drying. A refrigerator with no door sat at one end, stuffed with dirty plastic-wrapped lumps of unknown identity. Myles rang the bell.

A voice from the other side of the door invited him to open it. Some subconscious reflex caused him to pat his jacket, feeling for his semiautomatic before venturing in. He could smell controlled substances. Stepping into the front room, he found Ms. Sunkist bent over a bucket of clay. Her forearms were caked to the elbows, her fingers working a gray lump. She stood up then and smiled at him as though he were a brother.

The woman who faced him could have been Together Dating Service's top selection for Eric Whittier. She was tanned and lean, as if she spent six months a year working in a sundrenched field. And the other six months chopping wood on the side of a mountain. The hem of her flowered skirt brushed boots that looked like they hadn't been removed since 1968. Long, straight dark hair, laced with silver, hung against her breasts. The shirt was some sort of gauze and Myles had no doubt that she was lacking a bra.

Cats or something swirled around her feet. On a bare wooden table behind her were at least a dozen candles and a glass jelly jar stuffed with neatly rolled joints. Fat ones. Myles's mother used to keep a candy dish on the living-room table, filled with Jordan almonds.

He was tempted to ask what it was really like in the old days. He calculated that he must have been in about third grade when this lady was doing mushrooms at Woodstock. Feeling as though *he* were the anachronism, Myles flashed his badge and gave her a big grin.

> *Man passeth away like a shadow.*
> —Psalm 144:4

The man had walked into Marsha Landry's life one October, twenty-three years ago, life being the Wagon Wheel Restaurant on Route 28, the road to Wolfeboro. He was staying in one of the cabins near Duncan Lake, one of the few campgrounds open year round. Preferring the cold to the black flies and tourists, he felt lucky to experience the area known as the foot of the White Mountains during its finest seasons. Early October was one of the finest. He had taken a week off from his job as a postman somewhere down in the Boston area and made his biannual pilgrimage north.

Sometimes he brought his wife, but this time he came alone. His hair was dark and short. Short for the late sixties era, but he had been a military man and was looking at middle age. His name was Ray.

Marsha was having problems with a customer who was giving her a hard time. At one point the man had raised his voice at her and then suddenly Ray was standing by the table. There was a brief scene, then as it was about to escalate the customer stood up and left.

Marsha was a bit embarrassed. She would have preferred to handle the customer with a dinner on the house, which usually worked. But his concern endeared him to her. She thanked him and he sat back down at his table. By the time he had finished dessert and coffee, which she neglected to add to the check, they had a date.

Marsha's shift ended at ten P.M. He had returned to the restaurant, freshly showered and after-shaved, to pick her up. They drove to Wolfeboro for a couple of drinks and a walk along the lake. Then, returning to the warmth of his car, and too eager to wait for the drive back to his cabin, they climbed into the backseat and Dover was conceived.

Except for her shifts, they spent every hour of the next week together. Marsha felt she came to know him intimately, better than anyone she had ever known. But on the last day, as she watched him drive off, she realized, of course, that she didn't know him at all.

"Not even his last name?" Dunn asked, when the story was finished.

"No. She used to say, 'Honey, you don't need a last name in the dark.' "

The friends and relatives of the deceased had trickled by, but except for a couple of curious glances, no one had dis-

turbed the two. Greenlawn Cemetery was empty now, empty
of the living.

"She knew he was married. He never made her any promises. She accepted all that. But she thought that she would
see him again, in the spring."

"Did she?"

"She never saw him again."

Her tears had dried by now, and she stood up. Dunn
walked her to her truck, parked in the next block down. He
asked as they strolled: "What made you think Bishop was
the man?"

"When Mom died three years ago, I had written down
everything she had ever told me, which hadn't been much.
I resolved then to find him."

"Why?" But he knew the answer.

"When she was alive, I didn't need to know who I was.
Or else, maybe, somehow I did know. When she died, I
didn't anymore. And needed to."

Dunn's head spun, but he understood.

"So I started searching, with very little to go on. Wrote
tons of letters and got tons of nowhere. She thought he had
said the north of Boston, so I concentrated there. Do you
know how many Rays there are working for the post offices
in the North Shore? Who were vets? But then I got an inspiration. I talked to the owner of the Duncan Lake Campground a few months ago. Inspiration doesn't come quickly
to me, I'm afraid."

Dunn thought, to many people it never comes.

She continued: "Of course, he didn't have records from
twenty years ago, but I knew the man had come up regularly,
really liked this area, and despite the risk of running into my
mother again, might venture up again. So I asked him if he
could remember someone of that description—someone who
occasionally brings a wife, someone from Massachusetts.
Who came only in the off-season."

They had reached the truck. The cold front was beginning to move in and Dunn could feel the temperature dropping. She shivered as the first of the gusts sought them out. But the story wasn't finished.

"Why don't you come back to the station with me? I could treat you to a nice can of nuked spaghetti."

The offer was too good to refuse, and she agreed. Twenty minutes later they sat in the small lunchroom letting the chill which had insidiously crept into their bodies melt away. In the end Dunn had actually opted for something resembling a pop-tart. He watched her push the small mushy spaghetti rings around with a plastic spoon and felt he had let her down.

"Well, eventually the Duncan Lake Campground paid off. I looked through most of the records myself, going back as many years as he had kept. The owner couldn't remember the name, but thought he knew someone who fit. That kept me going. A couple months ago I found it. Ray Bishop. Sometimes, Mr. and Mrs., from Salem, Mass. Ross, the owner, remembered the car after I came up with the name. Big Lincoln, with a bumper sticker, America—Love it or Leave it. I figured he had to be a vet. But I wrote and got confirmation, also that he worked for the post office. That's when I came done here. Got a room and a job in Beverly."

"Did you contact him?"

"You know, for three years I thought about the moment when I would have a name and address in front of me, how I would pick up the phone, jump in the truck, take off for the past, face it good or bad, so I could come back home to the present. Get on with my life. But I stared at the piece of paper every night for months. Postponing the confrontation."

"Why?"

"I'd like to say I had second thoughts about disrupting his life and hurting his family. But that wasn't really it. I was scared."

Dunn smiled. At least she was honest. But oh, so young.

She continued with the exuberant self-analysis that you must go through constantly when young, until a family of your own forces you to grow up and be that person most of the day. Self-examination is relegated to your third day of vacation, or the wee hours of the morning when you can't sleep, or after a fight with your spouse, or for weddings, or for funerals.

She was afraid, of course, of what she'd find. A man less handsome, less heroic than her mother had known. He had, after all, abandoned the mother of his child, yet for one week, he had made her happier than she had ever been. Marsha Landry had never expressed bitterness, but Dover felt it for the first time at her mother's funeral, when the last opportunity for the fairy tale to have a happy ending had crumbled like ashes. Dover was afraid of Bishop's rejecting her, but mostly she was afraid of what she'd feel toward him.

For a moment, it occurred to Dunn that she could be holding back a tiny bit. What if the foot-dragging had ended three weeks ago? What if she *had* confronted Bishop, and that all her worst fears had been confirmed? This was a determined young woman, with a rugged, protective quality that permeated the telling of her mother's story. Her arms were slender, but the muscles defined. Could she kill with one blow? Could she kill for her mother's broken heart? Were her tears at the funeral tears of guilt?

Dunn asked: "So you never met him? Never contacted him?"

"No. I've never even seen a picture. The next thing was, I saw the article and obituary in Tuesday's paper, and decided to come to the funeral. Never said hello, at least I could say good-bye."

"You seemed to be saying more than that," he said. He

pushed back his chair and walked over to the coffee machine. "Coffee?" he asked her.

She waited until he had returned with the cups before answering. "I didn't expect it to hit me like that. A complete stranger being lowered into the ground, a face I had never known, never will. Never will hear his voice. But suddenly I felt like twenty-three years of emotions you feel toward your father, or that I imagine you feel, came forth, needing to be felt before the earth swallowed him up. I felt a kind of release, an ending. But also immense grief. She loved him. We loved him. I was grieving because I had just lost the father I never had."

"What do you do now?"

"I don't know," she responded, cradling her coffee.

"Would you like to see a picture?" he asked. There was a good one that Coleen had given Jake during the missing-person investigation. A softer image than the more recent shot they had been dragging around to witnesses. They went up to the office and he fished it from the pile on top of his desk. She stared at it quietly for a few minutes, then said: "I feel selfish . . . I think I really need to know for sure. I've come this far, what if it's not him? I expected all this time that one way or another, I'd get confirmation from him. He can't give it to me now."

"Do you want to meet his wife? If he was your father, she could tell you about him."

"I would, yes. But I can't bring myself to upset her at a time like this. She's entitled to her memories, and to privacy right now."

"You're entitled, too. You're entitled to the truth. Coleen Bishop was not the wronged wife, she married Bishop only six years ago. Your mother was well before Coleen's time. I don't think she will be too upset about it."

Her eyes began to shine. "She may be able to help me." Her words sounded like those of a child. She felt adrift. Lost

in space. Is it better to lose someone you love than to not
know if you've lost someone?

"Then you should talk to her."

Not every interview yielded him a clue to the murder. But
each relinquished a clue to life.

Chapter 20

Quantus tremor est futurus,
Quando Judex est venturus,
Cuncta stricte discussurus!

What a terror is in store
when the Judge shall arrive
and all knots shall be unravelled!
—Requiem "Dies irae"

Friday, shortly after one in the afternoon, Dunn's phone rang. It was Myles on the car phone. A woman named Portia Sunkist had confirmed Whittier's alibi.

"You can forget Sunday. I grilled her. Their tables were side by side. Until late Sunday night, he was never out of sight more than a few minutes."

"OK. How about Saturday?"

"Whittier drove to Portia's place around five Saturday evening. They had something to eat there, then they went down to Salem for a movie."

"East India Mall?" Dunn asked.

"What d'ya take them for? A foreign flick at the college. Ran from about eight to about nine-thirty. I checked."

"He never left her side?"

"I really pressed her. After a great deal of effort and a lot of kneading of clay, she remembered two times Saturday. She offered me a piece of clay while she was thinking."

151

"To eat?"

"No. To knead. She said it would help me."

"Help you what?"

"Tension. Karma. I wasn't all that clear. Gabe, this lady still says stuff like 'far out.' Anyway, Whittier left the movie for a couple minutes. Said he had to make a phone call."

"Did he say who he was calling?" Dunn asked.

"Nope. Anyway, the second time, they went up Lafayette to a sub shop for coffee after the movie. He went to the men's room and was gone maybe fifteen minutes. When he came back to the table, he said he had felt ill, but was all better. She blamed it on the dinner she had served him."

"Which was . . ."

"I didn't ask. You should have seen her kitchen. I wouldn't be surprised if it was eye of newt. But my gut feeling is that dinner was irrelevant."

"I think I agree. How far is the sub shop from the Willows, would you say? Five or ten minutes?"

"Not enough time, is it?" Myles said.

"How about Forest River Park?"

The phone was quiet for a minute. Myles whistled. "Two blocks. I wasn't thinking of that."

"Neither was I, until just now. And afterward?"

"They went straight to bed. Hers. He made damn sure she'd remember him."

Dunn smiled. "Far out."

Denn alles Fleisch
es ist wie Gras.

All flesh is as the grass.
—Peter 1:24

After being outside the better part of the morning, Coleen felt the kitchen to be stuffy and hot. Her sister was unloading the dishwasher and the clatter of glasses grated on Coleen's undefended nerves. Somewhere in the past week she had lost her entire epidermis, as if Ray's fate had inflicted her with third-degree burns. Good or bad, a marriage is a protective layer of sorts. The world fears you less, taunts you less, believes you more. You're a member of the club. Coleen felt that the heat in the kitchen was intensifying the pain from her burns. She stood up and opened a window.

"Would you like me to come over tomorrow and help you go through his things?" her sister asked from the sink. Ray had been *him* all week.

"No, thanks. I'm not ready yet." She wanted to be packed in a tub of ice. The numbness was wearing off and she longed for a bit more. "Angela," she said after a while. "The money you've been keeping for me?"

"Yes?"

"I think I may as well put it back in the bank."

"Yes, you should. Like I told you, I would have helped you out if you ever got stuck. You didn't have to worry."

"I know, Angela, but it made me feel . . . freer, somehow. To be able to just leave, and not depend on anyone."

"Wouldn't have lasted for very long," her sister said.

Maybe not, thought Coleen. But for a few days she wouldn't have needed either of them. She closed the window.

Later Friday afternoon, Dunn was in the lunchroom making a fresh pot of coffee. As he was sweeping up the half packet of grounds that had exploded onto the counter, Myles came in. The suggestion on the packet that one should *tear here* was a practical joke.

"You inquired about a dog, sir?" Myles asked. Behind him was a man in his thirties, wearing tan chinos and a high-school hockey jacket. Dunn looked over his shoulder and finished pouring in the water. "Well, Mr. Hank Terell here has come to tell you all about it."

Dunn wiped a hand off and extended it. "Mr. Terell."

The man shook his hand and began: "The officer here told me they had heard the Bishop dog was killed in an auto accident, and did I know anything about it. I told him yes, I did. It *was* hit by a car. That street's awful, you know."

"Yes, I know," Dunn said.

"Anyway, I was home that day . . ."

"What day was that?" Dunn asked.

"Right before Christmas. I had the day off, musta been the twenty-second or twenty-third. It was late in the afternoon, just starting to get dark. Ray had just come home and, well, I guess he took the dog out. He sometimes lets it off the leash. Dog's usually pretty good. But this time I guess it saw something across the street it couldn't pass up. Now I didn't actually see what happened, but I could sure hear it . . . the screech of tires. Car musta been going pretty fast, from the sound. Then I heard the dog. A horrible sound, just horrible. Then the dog was quiet. I could hear the car speed up. I was looking out the window by then. Then I ran out front. Ashamed to say, I didn't get the plate on it. Cream-colored sedan is all I noticed. No one from the neighborhood. And Ray, I'm sure he didn't get the plate, either. He was sitting in the street cradling the dog."

Dunn and Myles glanced at each other. Ray Bishop? Dunn thanked Mr. Terell for coming in. "Did you know Bishop?" he asked as Myles was walking the man to the door. Mr. Terell turned to face him.

"Ray? Yeah, a bit. He was all right once you got to know him." The man smiled and left. Salem High School, his last words in yellow on his back.

All right. The most glowing praise the detective had heard in five days.

When Myles came back, Dunn asked: "How many friends

and relatives have we questioned, Jake? Finally we find someone for whom Ray was 'all right.' "

"Why didn't Bishop go after the car?" Myles asked.

Dunn said grimly: "He had already been warned about the leash law, remember. The sedan may have been the executioner, but Bishop did the sentencing when he let that dog loose. I can understand why he didn't want to talk to Coleen about it. But it might have helped them both if he had."

> On the willows there
> We hung up our lives
> For our captors there
> Required
> Of us songs
> —Stephen Schwartz, *Godspell*

When Dunn was a sophomore at Salem High he went out with a girl named Alice from Juniper Point. Long after they broke up, he still hung out with her brothers, remaining an honorary member of the Willows Boys, a local, and to the cops, crazy but benevolent gang. The Willows Boys usually hung around down at the line, even during weather that forced most primates to remain indoors. When they weren't defending their territory from the Danvers and Beverly kids, they were up in the giant copper beech that spread from the men's to the ladies' cottages and beyond, so old and enormous were its branches. And high. The uppermost limbs lifted you up and out of Salem, into space.

They played Beat the Bastard in the copper beech every night of the summer. Those days they used a plastic bat, but the story was that someone's cousin, or the cousin's friend from Swampscott, had been hit with a real bat once and had died, or was spending the rest of his life in Bridgewater, or went on to become mayor. Dunn hadn't seen it, nor had Alice's brothers. But they knew a guy who had been there.

The line was a real jumpin' place back then. The rides were still in there, back before public safety was invented. The original carousel was down at the end, overlooking the water, with its famous Flying Horses, the oldest in New England, now flying in some museum. Dunn worked the carousel one summer before they were retired, or put to pasture.

One of the younger kids in the gang, well after Dunn's time, had taken a few wrong turns and dropped out of high school. Dunn didn't know him well, only by sight and reputation. The kid's name was David Morris.

David had done some time and was out on parole one summer when Dunn was still in uniform and backing up the twenty-one-car during the July Fourth weekend. Vans had lined Monument Road that day where it led into the park. Clumps of teenagers had been hanging about the open doors, and on the low wall demarcating the beach. Closer in, the teenagers had given way to families, spread out over the grass with precarious camping tables, loaded coolers, and barbecues. Hibachis, folding chairs, grocery bags, and radios. One or more in every group drowning out the neighbors' music or the whining kids, creating a campfire sort of peace.

There was a new guy on the force, Officer Joe Bader, who had transferred from the Registry police a year earlier. He was working the twenty-one-car day shift that weekend. The guy was a little high and mighty for Dunn's tastes. And a bit short-fused.

Bader was down by the public beach checking out the crowd. Dunn was in his cruiser at the opposite end of the park. Between them were a thousand people enjoying the holiday, a wall of willow trees, and a volleyball game in the clearing across from the beach. Even back then, there was a law on the books outlawing the consumption of alcoholic beverages in the park. Officer Bader's mission was to uphold the law. And there was David Morris sitting on the low beach wall in a pair of cutoffs, no shirt, and a can of Budweiser in his hand. Bader didn't know Morris was on parole, not that he would have cared. Morris didn't know about the law, nor would he have cared. Except this summer he cared.

Bader approached the youth. "Hey, kid, would you come over here, please? You know it's against the law to drink down here." He reached for his handcuffs. "Afraid I'm going to have to take you down to the station."

David Morris froze for one brief second in disbelief and then in terror. Any other cop would have given him a warning. Many would have looked the other way, or said quietly: "Listen, pal, don't make me look bad in front of all these people. For chrissake, stick it in a bag, would ya? Or a paper cup!" But there was Bader unsnapping the cuffs.

For David there was only one response. He bolted. Tore off through the crowds, darting around hibachis, pushing aside the cascading leaves of the weeping willows. Kids and seagulls scattered in his path. Silver-haired heads turned, and heads with earphones. Aluminum chairs strained, spatulas hung frozen in midair, the volleyball bounced unnoticed out of bounds and onto the sand. David ran between the men's and ladies' cottages, ducking the low-lying branches of the copper beech, no longer able to save him from the Bastard. This game he had to win. And so he ran. Officer Bader pounding on foot behind him, blinded with sweat, adrenaline cranked up as high as it would go, screaming into his portable radio for backup.

Dunn heard the call and stepped out of the car, just in time to see David Morris flying down the hill toward him. Catching sight of the steaming patrolman in the distance, Dunn reached out a hand and beckoned to the boy.

"You better come with me, kid," he yelled as David came within earshot. The boy slowed, glancing fearfully over his shoulder and from side to side, weighing his options. Dunn continued: "The way he's worked up now, you could get hurt. It's me or him."

David stopped and turned desperate eyes toward him. Something in Dunn's look tipped the balance. The boy turned and headed in his direction. By the time he reached the cruiser he was sobbing. "One fucking beer and he comes after me. One fucking beer. I just got out of prison. I can't go back in there. I can't go back." The will to resist drained from his limbs and soul. Dunn leaned him gently but firmly against the cruiser, patted him down, what little there was to pat, and cuffed him. Asshole, he thought. Who'd chase a kid for one lousy beer?

Bader never slowed. Before Dunn had a chance to get the boy into the car, Bader appeared from nowhere, in full nuclear meltdown, headed straight for David, and began wailing on him, pounding with full fury as David, manacled and defenseless, collapsed to his knees in surrender. Dunn grabbed Bader around the neck and hauled back as hard as he could. It took all he had to pry the cop off.

David Morris was taken to the station alive. Before bringing the boy inside, Dunn handed him a mashed-up Dunkin' Donuts napkin for his nose. Dunn took care of booking him, and stayed with him till he was safely in a cell. "Sorry, David," he said before he left. "It shouldn't have happened that way. Cops get a little crazy when they chase people. Can I get you anything?"

The kid shook his head. His upper lip was swollen and caked with blood. After the warm sunshine the cell felt cold. His belt and shoes were in a laundry basket out in the hall. He had declined his phone call. Dunn handed him a blanket and left.

The next morning the court released him on personal recognizance. His trial date wasn't for a couple of weeks, but with the resisting-arrest charge, Dunn knew the boy had violated his parole sufficiently to go back in.

Two days later, shortly after sunrise, the beat officer on the twelve to eight A.M. shift found David Morris in the copper beech. No note.

The knot in Dunn's stomach remained for years. They say the job changes you. But it wasn't the job. It was the people.

Dover waited until evening, until she thought Mrs. Bishop had rested from the last of her visitors. She had parked her truck in Pickering Wharf and wandered around the stores for a couple of hours, killing time. Several times she had stopped at flower shops, and considered what arrangement would be most appropriate to bring. In the end, they all seemed sadly inadequate to her and she showed up at the door empty-handed.

Dover realized as soon as she had been invited in that her story could sound like the classic missing-heir-shows-up-at-funeral deal, ready to claim a share of the estate or to break the will. Suddenly she felt immensely embarrassed and wished she hadn't come. She had no place in this poor woman's house, and, as she took a seat on the edge of the sofa, felt somehow that she contaminated the room. If she had only brought flowers, after all, she could have made up some quick thing like, "I knew your husband, met him once. He paid me a small kindness I shall never forget. I wanted to remember him with these violets and to let you know my thoughts are with you. Good night, I won't keep you." What small kindness? *He fucked my mother.* "He let me in ahead of him at Stop and Shop. You see, the line was nine people long, each with full carts, and I only had a package of processed cheese."

But she didn't. She stayed and faced Coleen. She explained her story briefly, hesitantly, leaving out the part about the car. "I could be entirely mistaken, I need to know for my own peace of mind." The words sounded so awful.

Talking to a new widow on the day of her husband's funeral about how important my *peace of mind is*, she thought.

Coleen heard the whole story without making a sound. When Dover had finished, the older woman stood up and came to sit beside her. Slipping an arm around the young girl's shoulders, she said in a voice that cracked: "I'm sorry you have made this journey for nothing. Ray was sterile. All his life."

Chapter 21

Esurientes implevit bonis.

He hath satisfied well the hungry.
—Luke 1:53

The Friday-evening traffic on Lafayette Street had congealed like cooked egg. Unable to see far enough ahead to determine the cause, if any, Dunn consoled himself with the bumper stickers surrounding him. There may well have been no cause at all. Often large herds of cars simply had minds of their own, out of reach and beyond the understanding of their individual drivers.

Since learning to drive, Dunn had forced himself to interpret bumper stickers as an exercise in reading, much as a foreigner would to practice his English. When he was stuck in traffic, it kept him from boiling over. And, of course, the gratification was immediate.

Firstly, it was important for the world to know your political, moral, and emotional leanings. Who or what you loved, and who or what you hated. It was important, too, to declare where you'd been. Where you ate, what your car had climbed.

The car in front of him was a small foreign compact. Not

161

surprisingly, the owner was a Democrat, a supporter of whales, hugs, and a nonsupporter of nuclear power. It announced, falsely, that a child was aboard. Such announcements were no longer to be taken literally, Dunn realized, meaning now more that the owner had the ability to procreate rather than an actual inventory of the contents of the car. A separate sticker saying Support Youth Hockey suggested the owner had procreated more than once. Or had never grown up.

The gentleman to his right, not in a legal lane, but a lane which proclaimed the driver to have guts, was not interested in whales. The pickup was topped with an ill-fitting but imaginative cap. The back of the cap was covered with dirt, into which had been etched, Clean Me by some good Samaritan. Two stickers graced his tail. One supporting a local bar, the other offering conservation advice: Save a Tree— Eat Beaver.

The foreign compact pulled smoothly and responsibly forward when its time came, then suddenly jerked to a stop to let in the truck. The pack inched forward. Whatever had lain ahead no longer held its interest. Finally, he reached Sally's dorm. The compact accelerated out of view.

Sally Matsamoto was hunched up in a blue terry-cloth robe at one end of the couch. Still suffering the effects of whatever she had come down with, she looked pale and tired.

"Miss Matsamoto," Dunn asked, conscious of the effects a day and a half on a bus would have had upon her, "could you tell me what you remember of Saturday, March third? You were baby-sitting for Annie Pellegro, according to our notes."

"I'll try. It was three weeks ago." She picked up an aspirin bottle from the coffee table, shook out a couple into her hand, brought them to her lips, and washed them down with 7-Up.

"It's very important. Tell us what time you arrived at the house and proceed from there."

"I must have got there around five o'clock, I think. I walked from the bus stop. Mr. Pellegro didn't have his car. There were a couple guys there. They were all going on a ski trip, including Mr. Pellegro. I stayed with Annie until Sunday night."

"Did anything during that time strike you as out of the ordinary?"

Sally thought for a moment, then said: "Well, Annie was bugging . . . acting pretty weird. Other than that, no."

"How was she weird?"

"She stayed curled up in a corner a lot, like she was frightened. I couldn't get her to do anything. Even took her outside for a while, to push her in the swing. That seemed to work, but then it got dark and the snow was getting heavier, so I brought her back in."

"What else did she do?"

"Let's see. I read to her a while. She usually likes that. We go through the comics in the paper whenever I'm over there."

Dunn recalled for a second the pleasure he had felt years ago when his older brother Stephen had read the comics to him. Accommodating to his dyslexia had taken Dunn many arduous years. This had prolonged the routine of being read aloud to until he was nearly twelve. Stephen drowned in a boating accident shortly before that time, a tragedy which splintered the family for all time. The role of comic reader then fell to his younger brother Archie. Sheer embarrassment subsequently drove Dunn to manage this task on his own and started him on his rocky climb toward self-sufficiency. He also found himself missing Stephen too much, resenting any attempts to fill the older boy's shoes. It was either learn to read the comics himself or give them up. He learned to read.

"Did that calm her?" he asked.

"I'm trying to remember. No, actually it didn't. They weren't the usual comics. Wrong paper for some reason. And Annie wasn't being very flexible."

Dunn continued: "About what time was it when you were out back?"

"Maybe five-thirty or six."

"Sally, think very carefully. Did you notice any signs of activity next door, at the Bishop home? Hear anything or see anything? Cars parked, or pulling in or out?"

"I didn't see anyone. No cars that I remember. 'Course the garage door was closed."

"You said it got dark while you were out there. Did you see any lights on over there?"

A slightly puzzled look overtook her face. She answered: "I remember there weren't any lights. I remember because it struck me as kinda strange . . ." She seemed to finally snag some memory that had been eluding her. "Strange, 'cause I could hear music."

Dunn leaned forward from his seat on the opposite couch. "Music?"

"The swing is back by the Bishops' garage. There's some kind of room over the garage, with a window right over the swing. The window was closed, of course, so I didn't hear it at first. Almost didn't hear it at all. It was real faint. Sounded like a radio."

"Did you notice any lights later?"

"No," she responded.

"What about the next day? Sunday."

"I don't remember anyone coming, or any signs that they were home. I managed to drag Annie out a couple times to get some fresh air. Pushed her around in the wheelbarrow and stuff. I remember still hearing the radio faintly, but I didn't think anything of it at the time. Figured someone had left it on, either forgot, or sometimes people turn them on so people think you're at home."

Dunn was quiet for a moment. "Annie was still upset Sunday?" Sally nodded. He continued: "What about her tape recorder? Did you try playing any of her tapes for her?"

"No, you know, I couldn't find the tape player anywhere," she said, eyes widened. "I meant to tell Mr. Pellegro when he got back."

"Did you?"

"Well, no. He had a friend with him, a woman. I thought I should make myself scarce. He paid me and I left."

"And you saw no one else while you were there?"

She took a long sip of 7-Up. "Oh, yeah. Some neighbor came by Sunday morning."

"Who?" Dunn asked.

"The woman who lives on the other side of the Bishops. Came by to borrow a screwdriver. She said her husband was out of town, the Bishops didn't answer, and she was desperate. She didn't have the right kind."

"What did she need it for?" Dunn shuddered, remembering Rachel's suggestion about the ice pick.

"She said she wanted to tape *Murder, She Wrote* that night, but her kid had stuffed dominoes in the VCR."

Dunn considered this with bemusement. Then he stood up and thanked the girl. "Get some rest. Would you give us a call if you think of anything else?" She nodded, giving a weak smile as though her head were about to break. He saw himself out.

Dunn looked at his watch and pulled back out onto Lafayette. He always imagined that if he had a bumper sticker it would probably say, Never Home, in his ex-wife's immortal words.

Later Friday night, Dunn returned to Central Street and immediately recognized the red pickup parked in front of the station. He pulled into a CID space and locked up the Camaro for the night. As he headed for the front door, he noticed the pickup was not empty. Dover Landry sat huddled in the dark. She rolled down the window as he approached.

"Can I see you a minute?" she asked.

He leaned in the window. "Sure. Let's go inside. It's freezing out here." When she nodded assent he opened her door, rolling up her window as she stepped out. "How long have you been waiting?" he asked.

"A while. The guy inside said you'd be back tonight." She paused and looked up the street. "Will I get a ticket if I park here?"

"I'll take care of it. Come on." He led her into the station, checked in with the desk, then herded her up the stairs.

A few minutes later, as they sipped rewarmed coffee in the office, she told him of her meeting with Mrs. Bishop. Dunn digested her words quietly. Her expression vacillated between pain and resignation. Finally, she asked: "What if she's lying? Or mistaken?"

Dunn thought for a moment. It was possible that the recently bereaved widow might feel threatened by another claim on the estate or perhaps by a claim on the reputation and bereavement itself. It could have been quite a shock to Mrs. Bishop. He thought it unlikely that she'd be mistaken about his recent medical history, but it was of course possible she had no certain knowledge of his past abilities or lack thereof. Finally, he asked: "Dover, what's your blood type?"

She looked stunned, then answered: "I don't know. I suppose I may have known once, but I've forgotten. Jesus, I guess I should have thought of that . . . you probably know his?"

"Bishop's was AB positive. Let's find out yours." He stood up and tossed out the styrofoam cup. "Blood-typing can't prove fathers, but sometimes it can rule them out. Let's go visit my friend at Salem Hospital."

As he opened the door for her, she asked: "I don't know my mother's either. Won't that matter?"

"There's a pretty good chance it won't."

Fifteen minutes later they were negotiating the quiet maze of halls leading to the hospital laboratory. A small reception area outside the door was empty. Dunn led Dover behind the counter and tapped on the lab door. After a moment it opened, and a short figure in a white coat looked out at him.

"Mickey on tonight?" Dunn asked.

"Yeah, come on in."

Mickey Dineen had worked at the hospital about three years and was frequently hired by the police to draw blood, usually in surroundings far less friendly than the lab cubicles. The man, in his late twenties, was loading tubes into a centri-fuge. Dunn approached him and exchanged some prerequisite basketball chatter.

"Mickey, I need to type this young lady's blood."

"Help yourself. The serum's in those brown bottles down at the end of that counter. Everything you need should be there. Choose your weapon." To Mickey's satisfaction, Dover shuddered.

Dunn drew a stool up for her. She half perched on it and watched while he rummaged through bottles and jars. The lab smelled like a lab, some unidentifiable chemical aroma permeating the room. She wondered as she breathed in, whether lab technicians who spent all their days here didn't end their lives partially embalmed. Mickey went back to his business and left them alone.

Dunn selected two of the bottles, labeled Serum B and Serum A and placed them on the counter behind Dover. Further searching netted him a glass slide, a sterile, dispos-able needle, two tiny pipettes, and a couple of cotton balls soaked with disinfectant. Taking her left hand in his, he swabbed her index finger with the cotton. While it dried, he prepared the slide with a drop from each bottle.

"Ready?" he asked. She nodded.

Dunn lifted her finger once again, and with a quick jab pricked it with the needle. With one of the pipettes he milked a couple of drops of blood, turned and deposited them on one end of the slide, mixing them in with one of the drops of serum. He repeated this with the other pipette, mixing the blood this time with the drop of serum at the other end of the slide. He picked up the slide and carefully agitated it from side to side for a moment before holding it up to the light.

"Technically, we should give this a half hour for accuracy, but if we're going to get clumping, it should happen in a couple minutes." They made small talk for about five minutes, steering as clear as possible from bloody topics.

Finally Dunn said: "Let's take a look." He leaned over and switched on a microscope so she could see more easily what he was talking about. She peered through the eye piece and he showed her how to focus. "Notice it's clear . . . no flakes. If your blood contained type B corpuscles you'd see clumping. The result of serum A agglutinating the cells."

He shifted the slide so that they could see the other end. "This is serum B. Look, still no clumping. So, no type A blood cells, either. Dover, your blood group is O, like half the population."

Dover tried to remember the ramifications of this, but hadn't found the need for this particular law since she had passed biology. Dunn saw her struggling and said: "Ray Bishop could not have been your father."

Dover stared at the cotton ball pressed against her fingertip, watching the alcohol evaporate. In a barely audible voice she said: "Thank you."

Chapter 22

Deposuit potentes de sede,
et exaltavit humiles.

*He hath deposed the mighty from their seat,
and exalted the humble and meek.*
—Luke 1:52

On Saturday Dunn felt an overpowering urge to fly. He had, for once, the necessary funds, a couple of hours to himself, no winds, and not the least, a desperate need to clear his mind. He called up the flight school in Beverly and found a ten A.M. slot in his instructor's schedule with an available Skyhawk to match.

It had been nearly a year since a knee injury sustained while pursuing a suspect had resulted in some time off from the force. Dunn had passed one of those hours taking an "intro" flight offered by one of the schools at Beverly Airport, and had been hooked immediately. Since then, however, bad weather, low salary, poor budgeting, and gusty weekends had delayed his training to below the threshold pace needed to make progress. He felt less competent now than that moment during the intro when the instructor said casually: "You take it." And he hadn't felt too competent then.

His instructor was called Zack. At 280 pounds, he made lessons in the cramped Cessna 150 an intimate experience. Remarkably, Zack had stuck with Dunn, chiding him about his infrequent visits and proclaiming him the longest presolo student in New England aviation history.

"So what case are we sick of this time, Gabe?" Zack asked him while Dunn started to preflight the plane. Prior to taking out the smaller craft, Zack generally requested his students not to top off the fuel tanks, lest it put them over gross weight.

"I don't want to talk about it. That's why I'm here." Dunn undid a tie-down, letting the rope fall to the ground.

While waiting for take-off he asked the instructor if they could swing south over Salem before heading for the practice area. "I'd like to take a look at Salem Willows from the air. How low can we go?" he asked.

"A thousand feet. We'll still be in the control zone so tell the tower your intentions when you're airborne."

They departed straight-out from Runway 16, and as soon as they cleared the treetops could see the gas tank and power company stacks directly in front of them. Leveling off at a thousand feet, they reached the Willows in a couple of minutes. Dunn crossed and started a shallow bank to the left for two slow circles over the peninsula. The Coast Guard hangar and lighthouse on Winter Island, connected by a causeway to the Willows, passed below them. Then the narrow lots on Juniper Point, giving way to the park, just beginning to show some green. Most of the trees were still bare, however, and Dunn could make out the orange hulls of the rowboats between the buildings. The gazebos, the open air theater with its rows of bleachers, the carousel, the cottages, all could be picked out from that altitude. As the park dissolved into no-man's-land, he picked up the eastern end of Monument Road, and was struck by the patterns of trails and paths crisscrossing the central core of the Willows, inaccessible and invisible from the road. The homes on Monument Road sprung into view, Pellegro, Bishop, Lufkis, and across the street he spotted Raider's dock.

"Watch the ball!" Zack barked. "You're making me uncomfortable." Dunn gave the plane enough left rudder to coordinate the turn, then scanned the rest of the instruments and swore under his breath. Still losing altitude in his turns, after nearly twenty hours of logged flying time. He pushed Bishop out of his mind and concentrated on the cockpit.

They turned northeast and headed up the coast for some airwork. Dunn looked down once more to take in the harbor below him. South of Winter Island lay the larger and richer headlands of Marblehead, gracing Salem with a picture-postcard view that seldom changed. Marblehead money had seen to that. Ironically her wealth and power had not been able to preserve her own sweeping view, which toward the north was saddled with her much poorer neighbor. The Electric Light District had built the power plant some forty years before, along what used to be the Willows' broadest beach, and alongside it, some years later, the South Essex Sewerage District had sited its primary treatment plant. The sprawling grounds of the local hospital, the squalor of the county jail, the not particularly beautiful campus of the state college, also had found homes in Salem, whose population's ability to defend itself had never recovered from the devastation of the witchcraft hysteria three hundred years ago. Like guards appointed to keep the city in perpetual bondage, the power station stacks could be seen for forty miles on a clear day. The property stretched over half a mile, boasted almost a dozen storage tanks and a mountain of coal. Salem's cross to bear, however, was also Marblehead's. From the multimillion-dollar homes on her northern shore, you couldn't see the jail or smell the sewerage plant. But the stacks of the power station scarred the view for rich and poor alike.

High above Plum Island, Zack punished Dunn with a half

hour of stall practice, tacky jokes about dead people, and a simulated engine failure. Dunn failed the latter by selecting a landing spot he had no hope of making. "Time's up, you're dead," Zack crowed. "You'd have been better off going back for the beach." Thoroughly demoralized, Dunn headed back to Beverly for what Zack fondly termed some "crash and go's."

As an escape, flying was guaranteed to do the job. If you didn't leave your mental baggage on the ground, it could kill you in the air. The effect, no matter how stressful the flight, was to leave Dunn intensely exhausted but refreshed when he landed. It was also humbling.

"Your airwork's improving," Zack said charitably when they had landed and reentered the terminal. "Just need a little consistency in your landings. Better keep your day job. When will I see you next? Never mind . . . I'll just have to track the obituaries." He roared with laughter at his own joke. Dunn glared at him and pulled out his checkbook.

Even before he had left the parking lot, the case was flooding back. But in a different order, with a new perspective. Dunn found himself automatically putting back-pressure on the steering wheel as he headed up the airport road, and reminded himself that the car was never going to break ground. For five minutes after every flight he had to relearn to drive. Stuffing a Schumann cassette into the tape deck, he turned south on Route 97. Then he reached over and switched it off again.

Dunn now knew who killed Ray Bishop.

Jake Myles had left a message on his answering machine when the detective returned home. On the second ring Myles answered, and hearing Dunn's voice, said: "The Webers have split."

"When?"

"This morning. I went by to check out their typewriter.

You know, dumber stunts have been pulled. I thought it was worth ruling out. Anyway, the place was empty. The landlord's upstairs and was willing to let me in. Furniture's still there, but most of the personal stuff—clothes, suitcases, and so forth—are gone. What do you wanna do?''

Dunn was quiet for a moment. ''Nothing. They're not our problem.''

''Shouldn't we call Army Intelligence? Get his jacket pulled . . .''

''Whose, Jake? Whose jacket? You said they never heard of Weber. Figuring out his real name's going to take a while. Anyway, it's Saturday. You know they never answer on weekends.'' He thought about what life must be like on the run, starting all over in some strange town. Waking up with a new name, fearful you wouldn't remember it, remember which persona you were at some critical moment in a dangerous masquerade. Every stranger, every crowd held the sudden possibility of recognition. Weber's past lay like a steel trap on a forest floor. Dunn remembered the fear in Lila Weber's eyes and thought, she must really love him. He wondered whose eyes they were now. ''We can call Monday. They won't get far, whoever the hell they are.''

There was a second message. Rachel had called, apparently from the train station. Stuck with no ride home and heavy packages, she had hoped to find him in. Dunn tried her home number and got no answer. The message was only twenty minutes old. He got back in the Chevy and headed downtown.

The pay phone outside of Filene's wasn't happy with Coleen's Canadian dime and spat it back. She tried another and released her breath when Eric finally answered the phone. She had rehearsed her words but now thought them better aired in person.

''Can we talk?'' she asked.

"Sure, Coleen. Talk."

"No, I mean, can I come up?"

"Come up."

She hung up. Realizing she hadn't eaten all day, she stopped in the Papa Gino's next door. She ordered an overcooked spaghetti dinner and a cold glass of rosé which made up for it. That should get her to Topsfield.

Chapter 23

Quia respexit
humilitatem ancillae suae.

*For he hath looked to
the lowliness of his handmaiden.*
                    —Luke 1:48

An early-morning battleground every weekday between the train commuters and the employees of the courthouse across the street, the commuter rail parking lot stands nearly empty on Saturdays. Dunn pulled into the bus lane and drove slowly down the length of the station. One car was live-parked, its bumper telling Dunn, Only You Can Prevent Mental Health.

Less than a half dozen people milled around. Judging by their postures Dunn guessed the next train was not due for a while. No sign of his sister, he turned the car and was about to accelerate when someone caught his eye.

Perched on a railing overlooking the platform was a vaguely familiar figure in black. She was plugged into a Walkman and reading a book. It took a minute for Dunn to realize she was the fifteen-year-old he had seen at Raider's on Monday. He pulled over and got out of the car.

175

"Miss Raider?" he asked her. He had to ask twice before she turned and removed her headphones.

"Hey," she said by way of universal and totally egalitarian greeting. Her feet were encased in tiny combat boots that looked like they were made by Mattel. Jeans in faded blue, the only spot of color on her, were held at the knees with safety pins. Better the knees than the ears, Dunn thought. Her black T-shirt said Megadeath with some appropriate graphic depiction. Like some cartoonist said: Nature's way of saying Do Not Touch.

"I'm Gabe Dunn, Salem Police. I don't think we actually met the other day."

"I'm Sara."

"You waiting for the train or for a ride?"

"The train to Boston. Anyway, I can walk home from here," she said for the record, lest he think her a wimp. It was about a mile to Monument Road. Dunn nodded solemnly. With shoes like those she could probably walk to Boston.

"Take the train a lot?" he asked.

"Just Saturdays. I have friends in Boston."

A glimmer of interest. Dunn leaned against her railing and asked: "Saturdays? Any chance you went in three weeks ago?"

"I go in every Saturday."

"What time, usually?" Dunn knew the trains were less frequent on weekends.

"Whenever I get up. It varies. I guess usually I get the one o'clock, or the two-oh-seven sometimes." Dunn looked at his watch. She did the same. It was one forty-five.

"Did you know Ray Bishop? Know who he was?"

She gave a wry smile. "Everyone on our street did."

"Why?"

"He was a dork." The words were not uttered but expelled. Each consonant emphasized, each vowel drawn out. "A total jerk. Every time he drove by our house he'd slow down like he was inspecting our grass." The last word was hissed.

He probably was, thought Dunn. "You knew his car, then?"

"Sure. The one with the flags and guns and shit on all his bumpers. Big silver Cadillac tank thing."

"Lincoln?"

"Yeah . . . Lincoln Continental."

Dunn recalled a passage on witnesses from the bible of criminal investigation:

"The female when young is intensely interested in the world as it reacts to her. She can be an excellent source of information because she observes with interest events intrinsically boring."

He felt it worth asking: "So three weeks ago, you would have been here about the same time?" She nodded. "No chance you remember seeing Bishop here? At the station, or on your train?" Pellegro had said four or five that afternoon.

She shook her head. He noticed that at the roots the black hair was light brown. She actually had a sweet face.

Disappointed but not surprised, Dunn thanked her and straightened up. "What are you listening to?" he asked as she repositioned her earphones.

"Amazing Mudshark," she answered. "Know them?"

"Ah, no." He smiled and turned toward his car. As he reached the driver's-side door she looked up suddenly from her book and shouted after him: "Saw his tank, though."

"What?"

"His car. The Lincoln. It was parked over there." She pointed down the first of the parking aisles.

Dunn could have kissed her.

> *Why can't I talk to her*
> *when she's all I need*
> —Everett Pendleton

Frank and Linda Wilson checked into the Bel-Air Motel just outside of Indianapolis. They had driven most of the night and all morning. Frank wanted to sleep a few hours and continue the drive later in the evening. Inside the room he sat down on one of two flowered beds and began pulling off his shoes and socks. Linda moved a suitcase onto the floor. She sat beside him.

"Tom, I can't do this anymore."

"Frank. It's Frank."

"It can't be worth all this!"

"You're not the one facing prison," he said.

"What am I facing then? Can you tell me?"

Wilson stood up and went to the window. He yanked the drapes shut. "What do you want me to do?" he said wearily.

"Call another lawyer. It's been thirty-six years, Tom. Things may have changed."

"I called a lawyer just a couple years ago, remember?"

"You got him out of the phone book. You got five minutes of free advice. Probably all it was worth."

He pulled his keys and wallet from his pocket and set them on the nightstand. "Well, now I'm wanted for another murder."

She didn't answer. She watched her husband as he undressed and climbed into bed. With a note of defiance he pulled the sheet up to his chin. The starch alone would ward off all pursuers. He hoped for a few hours, anyway.

Lila leaned over to shut off the light. The drapes actually

darkened the room pretty well. She sat back, fully clothed, and stared at the ceiling. "Sweetheart, did you kill that postman?"

"No, dear."

After several minutes Lila began to laugh.

Chapter 24

Quidquid latet, apparebit.

That which is hidden shall appear.
—Requiem "Dies irae"

On the second visit to Walter Pellegro's house, Dunn brought a search warrant. The last time he had needed a warrant on a Saturday he had pulled Judge Harkness out of a church Bingo game. This time, thankfully, the clerk on call had been home. Probable cause had not been easy to establish. Dunn had to base his argument more on Pellegro's "consciousness of guilt," evidence that the suspect had lied with no apparent reason. The clerk was not impressed by the mercurial musical habits of Pellegro's daughter. Dunn knew better than to press it. He stuck to the car. After he laid out his case and itemized what he intended to look for, the clerk gave him what he needed.

Hurd and Myles accompanied him to Pellegro's. After the formalities the three men began to move about the house. They started with the living room and hall closet while Pellegro stood stiffly and watched them. The living room held no secrets, or held them well. The floors looked scrubbed and empty. Myles checked the underside of the coffee table with a flashlight. Rhythmic sounds of Annie's swing were discernible from the backyard.

The closet, on the other hand, was packed with life. Snow pants, boots, quilted snowsuits of sizes long outgrown, took up precious space. The correct sizes were there as well. At least Annie looked well cared for. Her father had saved a few inches for himself, and Dunn located outerwear for every season. He felt through the pockets of what looked to be Pellegro's winter jacket. One contained a lift ticket dated March 4. The plaid coat had numerous stains, none obviously blood, but he couldn't be sure. He pulled it off the hook and handed it to Myles. "Bag this for the lab, Jake."

Carefully they checked each room. Anything that matched the requirements of the murder weapon was wrapped and removed for lab analysis. Carpets were checked for stains. Pellegro watched silently and did nothing to stop them. Finally Dunn entered Annie's room and was thankful the child was outside. Most people reacted strongly to such an invasion of their privacy, even those who could understand the justification. For Annie there was no justification.

The room was cluttered but not unclean. A number of toys and books, most untouched, lined a set of shelves by her bed. The floor was strewn with cassette tapes and clothes, a wind-up music box, and assorted felt-tipped markers. The window faced the street, and, he noticed, had a good view of Bishop's stockade fence. Over the top, at the end closest to the sidewalk, Dunn could make out the rounded top of the imposing white gas tank, situated across the cove.

As he was about to leave, his glance fell on the hook dangling from the edge of the door. Apparently there were occasions when Pellegro did not want Annie to have free rein of the house. Dunn began to wonder what, if anything, she might be able to see or hear from her room with the door closed. His eyes traced its contours as he slowly moved to shut it. There was a liberal gap at the bottom, suggesting that when it was originally hung, the room had been carpeted, probably wall-to-wall. Dunn got down on his hands and knees and put his head to the floor. By pressing his cheek down, he had a good view of feet in the living room, and even if he had been hard of hearing, sounds carried as clearly as when the door was open. Dunn picked himself up and reached for the doorknob when suddenly he noticed something else. For one moment he stopped breathing. "Jake, get some tools in here. We're taking the door." Halfway up the back, the side which invariably was hidden against the bedroom wall except when Annie was locked alone within, were two faint, bloody handprints. The uncovered signature of a mute child's desperation, they told another tale as well.

> Olim lacus colueram,
> olim pulcher extiteram
> dum cignus ego fueram.
>
> > *Once I dwelt in lakes,*
> > *once I lived in beauty—*
> > *that was when I was a swan.*
> > —Carl Orff, *Carmina Burana*

Directly across the street from Walter Pellegro's house was Camp Naumkeag, a city-owned site along the edge of Collins Cove boasting a couple of wooden summer cottages, a flagpole, and playground. Various civic organizations rented the camp for summer events, and the school and recreation departments utilized it whenever the weather warranted. Locally it was known as the Girl Scout Camp.

Pellegro's water view, for which he paid dearly when he moved in four years ago, lay just to the left of the larger Naumkeag cottage. Enough of a slice to catch the dazzling reflections of the sun on the water in the late summer. At low tide he and Annie could see the sea gulls from her window diving and climbing over and over again with mussels for smashing on the rocks below. During high tides they had seen more colors of water than he dreamed the spectrum could contain. Every shade of gray, and white in the winter and black at night, streaked with the reflections of a hundred harbor lights. Every shade of blue, from slate blue, deep and dark on the coldest days in February, to teal in the summer, scored by the wakes of water skis. Early dawns on school days when he had to get Annie ready for the bus he discovered the violets and flame reds of the sea.

In August, as he sat on the stoop with a cold beer to his lips, he watched the water transform to silver, just as the sun began to set. So white he had to avert his eyes. So intense his heart would pound. Mortgaged to the hilt, this, his first house, still gave him tremendous satisfaction, his first perception of control in his life and peace in his surroundings.

One of his first investments when he moved to Salem had been a pair of binoculars. Never having known in his life one bird from another, or caring, he had begun to find excitement in spotting something new, if unnamed, each season. He often held them up to Annie's eyes but didn't know how to aim them, nor fathom what she saw. Still, she seemed to delight in the sharing.

Early the past spring was the first time he spied the swans, and he was shocked and thrilled. He ran into the kitchen for a handful of bread. Bread he had rejected that morning for its initial green spotting, bread Annie had rejected, too, on some more general and elusive esthetic principle. The swans would be hungrier. He went out the back door to pry his daughter from her swing. She sensed his urgency and did not complain. Together they crossed the street and climbed down to the beach behind the camp. Swans are greedy and mean, but very, very cool. They spotted the waving bread almost immediately, changed course, and headed toward the beach. But they refused to alter speed to any ungraceful rate. Annie went wild, to a degree seldom seen when she was without music. Pellegro became infected with her excitement. He watched her face and felt happy. The swans were blessed with her eye contact the way he rarely could be. He turned to the undeserving birds and then understood. Selfish they might be, but their physical beauty was generous beyond words, their grace and dignity symphonic.

Late that summer Ray Bishop erected a six-foot stockade fence between the two properties. The Pellegros awoke one morning in August and found their view, their water, their gulls were gone.

Chapter 25

Pleni sunt coeli et terra
gloria tua.

Filled are heaven and earth
with your glory.
—Requiem "Sanctus"

Dunn picked up the phone and dialed Gloria Mei's home number. When she answered, he asked: "Gloria, you have the results of the stomach contents yet?"

"Are you approving overtime on this?" she asked incredulously.

"Just today. Just Jake's and mine, unless we make an arrest. So I want to wrap it up. I'm not working for free tomorrow."

"But I'm supposed to today?"

"C'mon, Gloria. I'll buy you lunch next time you get a lunch break."

She laughed. "Actually I sent it over yesterday. You should have it Monday. But if it's any help, contents contained pieces of undigested pork, Chinese-style pork. And bits of orange peel."

Weylu's, Dunn thought. *The bastard died Friday night.* And the mail inside the door Monday had lain there two

days, because Bishop wasn't alive Saturday afternoon to pick
it up from the floor. The clock radio would have come on
at its appointed time Saturday morning.

"Thanks, Gloria. You name the place."

"Not McDonald's, and not Chinese." She hung up.

Mihi quoque spem dedisti.

Thou hast given hope to me as well.
—Requiem "Dies irae"

Weber had gotten up for a drink of water. When he returned Lila rolled onto her side and faced him. She hadn't
slept. How could they confront the future if they couldn't
confront the past?

"Tom?"

"Mmmh?" He sat down on the edge of the bed, cradling
his glass.

She reached out and put a hand on his leg. "Let's go
home," she whispered. "Let's go home."

*He had wanted to be a hero. He was only trying to help
her. To be a hero for her. The guy was slapping her around,
viciously, mercilessly. Weber, né Wiley, didn't know any Korean, so he couldn't know what the fight was about. Couldn't
know what was worth doing this to another human being.
Especially a ninety-pound woman. Barely a woman, a girl.
The man was smaller than Wiley, but twice as strong. And
crazy. Oblivious to Wiley's intrusion. Unstoppable as a tank.*

The guy was fucking strong.

But Wiley was fucking armed.

*Unfortunately, it didn't turn out right. The girl was upset,
to put it mildly, when her man was wasted. And there were
witnesses. Witnesses who saw an American soldier gun down*

an unarmed Korean on his native soil. High Noon *this was not.*

Condemned and ashamed, Wiley took flight, carrying only his weapon and his remorse. The split second in your life you would give all the rest to take back. But you can't. And so it never ends.

Eric didn't answer at the house, so Coleen went back to the barn where she supposed he'd be working. She let herself in the side door and called out his name. Stepping into the center of the workshop she surveyed for a moment the assemblage of work, completed and uncompleted, that lined the perimeter. Panes of uncut mirrored glass were interspersed with window frames and pieces of leaded glass. Propped on the floor and leaning against the walls and benches, the angular images distorted the chamber. Reflections of her red raincoat spattered the muted grays and browns of the dusk-shrouded room like so many wounds. With each step, each turn, the shapes would disappear and reappear somewhere else. Coleen felt she was standing in a kaleidoscope.

She called again, louder. This time she heard a door creak open and from the storeroom at the back of the barn he emerged. Bathed in the light from the doorway behind him, Eric walked out to her, a roll of wire in one hand and a glass cutter in the other. At his wordless approach, Coleen suddenly felt she no longer recognized the man. An icy knot tightened in the back of her neck.

Dunn began to pace the station. The alibi was no longer a problem. But he had no weapon, and not much of a motive. All he could do now was wait for the state. From his first arrival on a scene to the last evidence transmittal form, it was ultimately the state that set the pace. *As it was in the beginning . . .*

Agitated, he took a walk downstairs to the garage. He

made a quick circle around the silver Lincoln, like some sort of rain dance. Some pieces were fitting, some were not.

Dunn moved to the storeroom off the garage where confiscated property was stored. At the moment, it held three motorcycles seized in various raids, a snowblower, a bank of chairs, and boxes of junk. And Annie's door, wrapped and waiting for the trip to Boston. It would be days before the lab would give him results, even unofficial ones. Dunn was severely tempted to call Mickey at the hospital. AB was pretty rare. If it was on the door, Mickey could find out in twenty-five minutes.

After making the rounds, Dunn went back up to the detectives' room where the evidence bag from Pellegro's house sat leaning against the water cooler, facing the same fate and delays as the door. He took it over to his desk. Then he opened the bag and pulled out the contents. Someone had transported the body to the park on a cold winter day or night. If that person had been Pellegro, he was likely to have worn this jacket. Dunn twisted the desk light so that it illuminated the coat. He lifted each cuff, then went over the rest looking for smears or splashes. The ones he found could have been any substance.

Both he and Myles had given the pockets a cursory check at the house. Dunn went through them again. Maybe they had missed the car keys, or the blunt instrument, he thought ruefully.

Three of them were zippered shut. They appeared to have been unused. One exterior breast pocket, and two inside the jacket. Exterior side pockets are always used, however, and Pellegro's were no exception. Dunn reached to pull the left pocket inside out. The flannel interior was grubby but not bloody. The lift ticket and a balled-up Kleenex dislodged themselves and fell to the table. Small woolly lumps that grow in all pockets held more tenaciously. Dunn patiently

separated each one with the blade of his knife, but unearthed
nothing.

The pocket on the right was less communicative. As Dunn
poked at the fluffy occupants he noticed an even more univer
sal feature—a small hole. The kind of hole you lose dimes
and keys in. Curious, he prodded the jacket lining carefully
from the pocket insert down to the hem. The stiffness of the
hem and the natural tendency of jacket lining to collect more
densely along the bottom edge caused him to nearly miss
what he had in fact missed in his quick search at the house
earlier. But this time he felt it.

The screw was an inch and a quarter in length. The green
paint had been scraped out of its slot, but still clung to the
head. Green, the color of murder.

Chapter 26

Libera me de ora leonis,
Ne cadam in obscurum,
Ne absorbeat me Tartarus.

Free me from the mouth of the lion,
And let me not fall into the darkness,
Nor hell engulf me.
                    —Requiem "Offertorium"

"Eric?" she said, finally. He gave her a smile which confused her. Hoping for reassurance she added: "You frightened me."

He put down his things and offered to take her coat. Coleen shivered and declined. "It's like ice in here. Eric, I have to ask you something."

Maybe the rosé was a mistake, she thought. *Maybe I should leave.* But she steeled herself and continued: "Did you blackmail Mr. Weber?"

Eric sat down on the stool and didn't respond.

"It had to have been you. You were the only one I told. I thought for a while it was Ray. But the police told me about your mortgage payment. And Ray wouldn't have done it."

"You think I would?"

"Where did you get the money?"

Eric got up and walked slowly around the workshop, fingering the edges of panes as he moved by them. Coleen winced the way she did when Ray would test kitchen knives for sharpness.

"I didn't have enough information to blackmail him. Nothing I could tell the authorities."

Coleen thought for a minute. "But Ray did. If you told Weber you were Ray, that would have been enough to scare him."

"Where I get my money is nobody's business. I'm not accused of anything. No crime's been reported, has it? And I doubt Weber's going to. Even if he does, how would they prove it was me? Ray is the obvious suspect, and he can't deny it now." He turned and faced her. "Let it go, Coleen."

The fear had passed, replaced by remorse and disgust. Coleen stared at his face, then turned and walked to the door.

"Where are you going?"

She used to say "Salem." "Coming to Topsfield," "going back to Salem." Now she opened the door and looked beyond the paddock to where her Escort was parked, the rosy sunset caught in its windshield. She buttoned her raincoat and rewrapped her muffler.

"Home."

> Lacrimosa dies illa
> *The day of weeping*
> —Requiem "Dies irae"

When Dunn called her, he didn't explain, just that he needed her to translate. And to stay with Annie until someone from the Department of Social Services could get there. Mel was standing under a streetlight at the entrance to the mobile home park when he drove up just after six P.M. Saturday. She climbed in without a word.

"I brought my Orff," she said when she was settled. Most of Mel's music collection had been through her classroom at one time or another. This particular tape had become one of Annie's favorites, so much so that Mel had made a duplicate for her to take home. The search of Pellegro's house had failed to turn up the copy, though the father had confirmed on Mel's last home visit that the child listened to it constantly. Now, on the backseat of Dunn's car, was a small cassette player.

The warrant for his arrest was based on circumstantial evidence only. Possibly solid enough to convict. But Dunn felt he had to break the man. Brian Hurd and Jake Myles pulled up in front of Pellegro's as he did, and the four of them walked to the door. Pellegro opened it and gave them a surprised look.

"May we step inside, Mr. Pellegro?"

Annie was curled up on the couch with a box of cereal. When she caught sight of Mel, she got up and slowly approached her. On Dunn's signal, Mel crouched down and inserted the tape.

"Mr. Pellegro," Hurd began in as clear a voice as he could muster, "we have here a warrant for your arrest . . ."

The music began to play. Annie, who had dropped down beside her, suddenly stood up and backed away. Mel looked up at her, then shrugged and signed, "What's wrong?" Annie responded by striking the edge of one hand against the palm of the other. "Annie's saying 'stop,' " Mel spoke and signed, more to Annie than to anyone else. Annie repeated the motion without taking her eyes off the cassette player, commanding it, willing it to be silent, but the music continued.

" 'You have the right to remain silent . . .' " Hurd continued, reading from the small blue card. But Pellegro wasn't listening. His eyes were on Annie.

Annie moved forward and bent down toward the recorder. Fingers jabbing at various bumps, she knew these things could be turned off. Dunn reached down and gently held her shoulders. Pulling her out of reach, he said to Mel, "Why? Ask her why."

The police officer persisted: " 'Anything you say can and will be used against you in court . . .' "

Mel leaned forward and tried to engage the child's eyes, but they were fixed toward the music. Moving into her field of view, Mel signed, "Why? Why stop?" The child was becoming extremely agitated and kept reaching for the recorder. One last time Mel signed, inches from Annie's face, *"Why?"*

Then Annie responded: "Hit." Only instead of moving one fist into the palm of her other hand, she held it up to her head. There was a long silence, and then Walter Pellegro started to sob.

" 'Having those rights in mind do you wish to talk to me now?' "

> Qua resurget ex favilla
> Judicandus homo reus.
>
> *When from glowing embers rises
> the guilty man to be judged . . .*
> —Requiem "Dies irae"

It was Annie who had let him in that Friday night. Were it not for that, the argument might have remained at the threshold. Raised voices, fires fueled, fists clenched impotently, separated by the invisible but powerful plane of the doorway that says *my house, my territory*. The lines would never have been crossed. But Pellegro had been in the basement transferring the week's worth of laundry from washer to dryer. So when the doorbell began to ring insistently, continuously, accompanied by loud pounding, Annie went to the door, opened it, and their neighbor stepped inside. Her father's footsteps flew up the stairs and into the living room. Bishop greeted him with reddened face, the stench of beer, and loud proclamations which Pellegro could hardly make out over the blaring of Annie's cassette player. The pointing finger made the words unnecessary, however. Pellegro had, once again and with some not-so-hidden malice, left the window nearest his neighbor's house slightly cracked. Since the outside temperature was in the twenties, this was at some loss of comfort and decided personal sacrifice to Pellegro and his daughter. He paid for this recurring message in this season's heat bills. In front of this particular window was poised the cassette player.

> semper crescis
> aut decrescis;
> vita detestabilis . . .
>
> *always rising*
> *and then falling;*
> *detestable life . . .*

The scene played itself out quickly. There was yelling, there were words and accusations, neighbor against neighbor.

nunc obdurat
et tunc curat
ludo mentis aciem,

> *now you are hard on us*
> *and then you care*
> *to amuse yourself by ap-*
> *peasing us,*

Bishop's emotions were swelled with drink. The Latin chanted forth from the speakers, taunting and defiant. Defiant as his wife's final, wordless glance as she walked out the front door twenty-four hours before. No argument, no shouting, no complaining. The front door closed behind her, the car door slammed, again and again his eyes filled now with the images of doors, and he heard them slam in the sounds of the bass drum.

egestatem,
potestatem
dissolvit ut glaciem.

> *poverty*
> *and power*
> *are melted like ice.*

In sickness and in health, in sickness and in health. She was supposed to *be* there. Bishop reeled toward the music, and bellowed at Walter Pellegro like a wounded animal. The music crashed around him like a net so that his words, drowned out in its cacophony, hung in the air disarmed. *Let the fucking bitch go. Let them all go to hell.*

nunc per ludum
dorsum nudum
fero tui sceleris.

> *now because of your games*
> *I offer my naked back*
> *to your evil sport.*

Ray Bishop had reached a full boil. As the orchestra swelled in raucous climax, he took three steps toward the box, and with a sudden sweep of his arm, sent it crashing into the middle of the room. Orff's final verse still hung in the air, but the ensuing, absolute silence was louder still.

quod per sortem
sternit fortem,
mecum omnes plangite!

> *since by the mere casting of lots*
> *the strong are crushed,*
> *weep, all, with me!*

The sea gull was carved, incongruously, out of onyx, hardly a stone indigenous to the North Shore. Variegated in white, almost translucent, it had an ethereal quality to it which lifted it from the clutter adorning the mantelpiece. It perched on the end closest to Pellegro now, and as rage overtook him, he suddenly felt it in his grasp. With one powerful movement, he smashed it down, not on a human head, but on a six-foot cedar stockade fence. The walls that had imprisoned him caved in before him and slumped with a thud at his feet. Annie screamed.

In the eerie silence, Bishop had seen the gull coming toward him slowly, frame by frame. But to a man who is paralyzed, no motion is slow enough. He never heard the scream, but in the fractional second preceding it, he remembered his first wife, Meredith, poring over the blueprints at his side. Meredith, steadfast, headstrong, whose personality had permeated every stud, every nail of their house. Meredith would have never left of her own will. Meredith would have stuck it out, as should Coleen. The house lasted, so should the wives. *Till death do us part,* they had said. Till death do us part.

Chapter 27

novo mundo reserat
faciem Aprilis;

> *The face of April*
> *reveals a new world.*
> —Carl Orff, *Carmina Burana*

Mel had seen the For Sale sign on the bungalow overlooking the cove on her last home visit to the Pellegros during the winter. It lay at the opposite end of Monument Road, farthest from the park. At last she had obtained financing, and closed, and felt blessed. Blessed with a stagnant housing market and condo glut throughout the region. Blessed with an anxious and desperate owner who came down in price enough to cross the line between dream and reality. Blessed with a competent and aggressive broker, who, despite showing up at each visit with an infant strapped to her back, had belied her image in the end. The negotiations were forceful and the offer unbudging.

Two days after the closing, Mel stood in the bare living room, unadorned but for the three tall windows framing the harbor. Her life lay in boxes stacked in the middle of each room, and for the moment an open suitcase and sleeping bag were the only signs she was living there. Until she finished painting and pulling up carpeting, gold, stained, and blasphemous against perfectly good hardwood flooring, Mel refused to open a box.

It was a Sunday and peaceful. With no Sunday paper delivery yet, she had gotten an early start. By late afternoon she had finished the first coat throughout the living room and was cleaning her brush and roller when Gabe Dunn's Chevy pulled into her driveway. Excited over her first visitor, this visitor in particular, she had the door open before his second foot had hit the ground. He slammed the car door and smiled at her. This was a social call.

"Would you care for a beer?" she asked as she closed the door behind him. She snapped open the lid of a small ice chest and invited him to fish out one of the green bottles swimming in the slush. "I get electricity tomorrow, if I behave."

Dunn fished one out, opened it, and wiped his hands on his jeans.

The tour of the house was short, due to its size and the absence of knickknacks and their accompanying histories. No photos on the mantelpiece or unusual posters on the walls. She refrained from the long monologue that the home inspector had engaged in, realizing that the fact of the doorways not being entirely square could not possibly fascinate anyone else. Finally they carried their beers out onto the back lawn, trading the smell of paint for the salty dampness of the sea. They sat together companionably on a low wall, sipping and talking about the gas tank directly opposite them on the far shore of the cove. The tank was the one blemish in her view, but was also the last blessing. It alone probably shaved fifty thousand dollars off the price of each home overlooking it. Without the tank, she wouldn't be here now. She laughed then, and related to Dunn the previous owner's helpful suggestion. *Get that nun to paint it, like Boston Gas did down in Dorchester. Mother Teresa?*

After a moment Dunn said: "Actually, I stopped by to ask if you want to go to a concert at Salem State tomorrow night."

Mel's eyes grew bright. "Sure. What are they doing?"

"Nothing as decadent as Orff. Berlioz's *Requiem*. Starts at eight, I think."

Mel inquired then about his work, now that the Bishop case was over.

"I've got a blackmail case I've almost wrapped up. And in my spare time I'm helping some kid find her father."

She asked about Annie. The *Salem Evening News* had given a sketchy but overly dramatic account of the confession and had not mentioned what was to become of the child when her father was led off to jail. Dunn said she'd been placed in foster care and should be returning to school in a few days. Mel couldn't help but wonder what the child had had to endure on the night of the murder. "Do you know what happened?" she asked, turning to him.

"I think we do now. Ray Bishop had gone over to complain about the radio being too loud, like he had many times in the past. Apparently the two guys had a long-standing dispute over a fence that Bishop built. It ended up blocking almost the whole view of the cove from Pellegro's place."

Mel looked out over the water. Once she had made up her mind to have a piece of the coast, if any of it remained affordable, she could not look objectively at any other property the realtor showed her. Houses far nicer and roomier than this one suddenly seemed landlocked. "What did the fence have to do with the radio?"

"Pellegro had tried every avenue available to him. Consulted the city building inspector and every other department down there. And finally even a lawyer. He tried friendly negotiation, but didn't get anywhere. Because of the angle of the property lines and the siting of Pellegro's house, the fence was pretty oppressive. The guy felt like a prisoner in his own yard. No water view, which certainly was a factor in what he originally paid for the place. All he could see was fence. Somebody else's fence. A constant reminder of just how little power he had over his own property. A single parent with a handicapped kid already has plenty of choices taken away from him in his life. Pellegro was suffering from some sort of growing desperation which he was finding harder and harder to contain.''

Dunn took a long sip and continued: ''So last fall he started a subtle counterattack, almost what you'd describe as passive-aggressive, I guess, only actually not so subtle and not so passive. He began cracking open the window over-looking Bishop's bedroom whenever Annie had her tape recorder cranked up.''

''And that's quite often. She turns it up to the point of distortion because of her hearing.''

''Right. Pellegro used to stuff ear protectors in his ears. Anyway, Bishop really went over about the noise, but I gather the agenda went far beyond that. Unfortunately, he had had a few beers and ended up smashing the radio. A pretty hostile act.''

''Cranking it up full blast and opening your window could be considered a hostile act, too,'' Mel said.

''True, but one for the police to handle. You have to be pretty careful what you do in another man's home. Pellegro responded with unpremeditated and somewhat justifiable rage. Crushing Bishop's skull with a stone bird was a rather excessive display, but he could almost have pleaded self-defense, possibly defense of habitation. At least he could have gotten off a lot easier if he hadn't hidden the body. If he had come forward immediately.''

''Why did he hide the body? And why so nearby?'' She jiggled her bottle and watched the last bit of foam appear, then disappear.

Dunn explained that Pellegro hadn't had a car. An accident

earlier in the week had tied it up in the shop awaiting some part. Bishop was killed just after nine P.M. and Pellegro had eight good hours of darkness to go through successive stages of panic and clarity.

"He wasn't thinking in terms of getting off lightly, or pleading out, or cutting deals. He was thinking of the Department of Social Services. He knew he would lose Annie if he were caught. His first thought was to get rid of the body, hopefully to delay its discovery long enough to obscure the time and circumstances of death and then to remove all traces from his house. He spent the rest of the night doing just that."

"If he didn't have a car, how did he get Bishop to the cottage?"

"A wheelbarrow. There are dirt bike trails crisscrossing the wooded area that stretches from Pellegro's house down to the park. Most of it is right-of-way owned by the power company, some of it is state-owned. There are even some ruins of an old fort back in there. Anyway, the whole area is unbuildable and secluded. So he pulled a trash bag over the head and shoulders and hefted the body into the barrow. He was able to work his way down the trails to the park, only four or five hundred yards away. He had plenty of time and there was no moon. The men's cottage was the first hiding spot he came to. He had thought enough to bring a small flashlight, and when he discovered the padlock, he also discovered the screws on the hasp were exposed. All he needed was a couple of turns with his pen-knife blade and he could yank the hasp right off the doorjamb. But then he figured that to avoid arousing the suspicion of some passerby he should replace the hasp when he left. So he bent down, found the screws where they had fallen, and stuffed them into his jacket pocket. Unfortunately, later on, when he went to put them back in, one of them had slipped through a hole in his pocket deep into the lining. He used his knife to give the other one a couple of twists to secure it, and it seemed to hold.''

"Where was Annie all this time?" Mel shivered.

"Annie, we know, must have witnessed the killing. She was crouched in a corner when Pellegro loaded the body into the wheelbarrow, but at some point, she tried to pick up the bird. He knew he'd have to clean up carefully when he got back from the park, but to contain the problem, he locked Annie in her room. Her pounding with bloodstained fists on the back of the door, the one spot he didn't think to check when he wiped everything clean, was his downfall.''

"How did Bishop's car get to the station?"

"Well, as he cleaned up, his mind began to clear more and more. Before dumping Bishop in the cottage, he had thought to remove the keys and wallet, possibly to make robbery look like the motive. When he felt his house was pretty free of traces, he went next door and let himself in to Bishop's.''

"Why?" Mel's eyes widened.

Dunn answered: ''It occurred to him that if evidence could point to Bishop leaving town, the police would delay searching for him. He wanted to be sure the TV was turned off, and the lights. He also checked the oven, stuff like that. Then the idea of moving the car struck him. Of course, if he had thought of it hours earlier, he could have used it to move the body somewhere else. Anyway, he locked up, started up the car, closed the garage doors after himself, and drove it to the station. Less than a mile's walk back. He even slipped over early Saturday morning and swiped Bishop's *Boston Globe* to delay suspicion and throw the timing of his disappearance off.''

"Just Saturday's?"

"He didn't care about Sunday. He had an alibi.''

Just then he reached inside his jacket. "Almost forgot—

I have something for you." It was a tape of *Carmina Burana*. "To replace yours."

She laughed. "You keeping mine as evidence?" But he didn't answer.

She studied the small box for a while, letting his story roll around in her mind. It was an RCA recording, a different performance. She was glad of that, and suspected it was intentional.

"This is all so crazy!" she said at last. "That a man could die over a fence!"

"Mel, most homicides turn out to be stuff like this. But Bishop didn't die just because he put up a fence. He died because Pellegro's life had become less and less bearable. Because of the quiet desperation a man can be driven to when there seems to be no defense, and no options anymore."

"I can't believe murder can be so . . . ordinary," she said.

Dunn drained the rest of his beer and stood up. "Murder is never ordinary."

She followed him out to his car. Standing in the driveway, their heads both turned to look out over the cove, as if drawn by the same force that pulled in the water twice each day. Mel's eyes riveted, and following her gaze, he saw what she saw. It was April 8 and the swans had returned.